I0668999

Just Call Me Darling

by

JP Barry

The Fall of Winters Trilogy, Book Two

Publishing History
First Edition, 2024
Trade Paperback ISBN 978-1-5092-5789-8
Digital ISBN 978-1-5092-5790-4

Previously Published Muse It Up Publishing 2020
The Fall of Winters Trilogy, Book Two
Published in the United States of America

Dedication

For my husband & daughter—Everything is limitless, especially you.

Chapter 1

Luca

The moment anyone hears the surname *Santino*, you're labeled a gangster. Period. Case closed. Career, professional affiliations, education—doesn't matter. All they see is you holding a smoking gun over some random dead body. Shaking the stereotype is totally useless. It's like pissing into the wind. Don't even bother wasting your good time, breath, or energy. God knows I've foolishly spent countless hours in pursuit of changing the minds of insignificant, judgmental morons.

Oh, and do yourself a favor. Don't attempt to find an insult I haven't already been called. Wop, dago, Guinea, goombah, Fredo (because I've always been viewed as the weaker son), greasy, slime ball, thug, low life, Guido—I could go on, but I'll stop there. You get the point. The funny part is, as fingers are being pointed in your direction and slurs are slung, the second they need help, who do you think they run to? *That's right.* My father, Frances "Frank" Santino, notorious head of one of New York's largest, oldest, and most powerful crime families. However, I'd be remiss if I didn't note the perks. Fear resides inside of most humans, driving them to do whatever you want, immediately, if not sooner. Nobody in their right mind will screw with you, *ever.* The foolish few who have, well, let's just say they didn't do it again.

Nevertheless, let me make one thing crystal clear. I love my family, and I always will, but the desire for more in life was often a driving force for me to never get mixed up with the wrong side of the law. The determination to be seen and respected as an upstanding member of the community pushed me through college and law school, earning the attention of Ally Newman of Newman and Associates LLP, one of the top firms in the state. With my diploma in hand, the ink barely dry, Ally reached out, making one hell of an offer to join her team. Turning my back, metaphorically speaking, on joining "the family business" didn't upset my parents or siblings at all.

They made their choices, and I, mine. A mutual, unspoken veneration existed between each member of the Santino clan. If anything, they bragged endlessly over my accomplishments inside and outside of the courtroom to anyone who'd listen. But, as much as my emotions might've differed internally, I'd always be Luca Santino. An Italian-American, Brooklyn native, complete with a thick New York accent, and dark Mediterranean features. A guy who never suffered from any unanswered needs or wants. Bottom line? I came from good stock, regardless of how they earned a buck.

After a few years of me working for Newman and Associates LLP, Ally made me her left-hand man. Though I was a strong litigator, she'd often keep me out of the courthouse and firmly planted behind a desk researching and digging up dirt on the opposing side of whatever case was stumping the others in the office. Initially, it sucked. Putting up a fight, the back and forth, the mounting tension, and the sleepless nights fueled my soul, but nowadays none of that mattered. I was good at exposing secrets and wasn't afraid to get my hands dirty.

Ally's right-hand man, or in this case, woman, was Jennifer Glick. That girl never smiled. She was intense, stressed out, and a beast of an attorney. She lived off coffee, cigarettes, and unpredictable problems to solve at a moment's notice. The harder and more complicated the situation, the better.

"Come on, Jenny," I begged, dramatically wringing my hands, and following her through the office.

"It's Jennifer. You've worked here for ten years. It's always been Jennifer. Not Jen. Nor Jenny. Jennifer. And, no. I refuse to sit idly by watching you and your womanizing ways hurt her again. You had your chance and blew it—royally," she said firmly, not stopping her movement through the hallway once.

"Hey." I lowered my voice, gently taking hold of her arm, and forcing her hip to pivot to gain face-to-face contact. "I care about her. A lot. I made one mistake. It was a stupid move, one I regret every single day. Be a friend. Help me out."

"No, *and* we're the farthest thing from friends, Luca. You'll mess with her head, get her to fall in love with you for a second time, and then, when some tall, leggy, blonde with fake boobs walks by, you'll throw Maddy away, crushing her. Guess who got to pick up the pieces last time you tossed her aside? Me. Pass. Besides, she's with someone else. Someone who doesn't treat her like crap. Someone who appreciates and wants her not for a day, but for forever." With a snap of her wrist, she released my hold. If looks could kill, she'd have murdered me sight on scene.

Jennifer wasn't what I'd consider attractive, but apparently, Ryan Glick thought she was. Hell, he even married her, bitch mode and all. Her exterior appearance was harsh and rather unflattering. Pin straight, parted down the middle, shoulder-length, ashy-blonde hair, ice-blue eyes, a sharp nose, and a pale complexion added to her severe appearance. She was of average height, and her gait was tragically rigid and masculine. Her posture was always impeccable. Every day she'd show up dressed in a power business suit with heels, accessorized with some fancy designer bag. She seldom laughed, but a certain softness resided deep within her soul. This trait rarely rose to the surface. I'd only witnessed it once or twice over the past decade. Perhaps one had to know her for that side to reveal itself.

From day one, Jennifer never liked me. She made sure her blatant disdain for me was recognized. If we were assigned to the same case, she'd have it well known she was in change. If I dared to fall out of compliance, she'd hand me my ass with a grin on her smug face. Chances were she wasn't always like this, but a woman in a courtroom had to remain unemotional. The moment a tear was shed or a voice was raised, their power vanished. As a young counselor, Jennifer probably trained herself to perpetually be on the defense. Now, she couldn't turn it off.

However, what Jennifer said wasn't a complete lie. Women never lasted long in my world. I'd hang out with one, screw her, then dump her, moving along to the next. My intentions weren't to do the same with Madison Langmore. I *really* did like her. Screw that. If I'm being completely honest, a crazy in love emotion sat in the pit of my stomach for her, but things got too intense too fast. Truthfully, it freaked me out.

We'd dated hot and heavy for about a year before the topic of marriage came up. The moment that happened, immediate ghosting on my part occurred. Then, the inevitable break-up occurred, which she had to have seen coming. A few days later, she and Jennifer saw me at a bar with some random girl who'd been eyeing me that morning at a coffeehouse. Stupidly, I went to their table to let them know I'd leave if my being there bothered them, but I walked away feeling worse because Madison simply smiled and suggested she wasn't upset with me at all.

"I wish you only the best, Luca. You deserve it," she said that night.

Those were her last words to me.

That was the thing about that girl—she was sweet and kind to a fault. She always found the silver lining for anything. She should've yelled, screamed, thrown a drink in my face, or made a gigantic scene, but she didn't. In fact, before we parted *she* hugged *me*. I'd hurt her, but she didn't appear mad at all. Her actions and words confused and stung me. How could she not have any emotions for me after the attached-at-the-hip year we'd shared? Did the time mean nothing? Did I mean nothing?

In all fairness, Madison may have forgiven me, but she sure as hell stayed far away from me, which sucked. Often, Ally called upon Looking Glass Consultants to do some dumpster diving or to take a few pictures. Basically, unearth things we legally couldn't. Madison's parents, Richard and Donna Langmore, owned the business. She and her brother, David, worked there as well. That's how we met.

One fine spring morning, this stunning beauty walked into my office, introduced herself, and sat down. We attempted to play off the initial mutual attraction, but it was tough. Nothing really happened between us except for some coy flirting and dozens of "accidental" body brushes. This frustrating dance continued for three long months. I'd make lame excuses to see her, and she the same. I have no idea what I was waiting for. Typically, making the first move never took me longer than forty-eight to seventy-two hours, but this time something felt different. My gut instincts urged me that I'd met *the one*, and nothing had prepared me for that. Fear of rejection sat in the pit of my stomach—a sensation on no occasion had I ever experienced. I'd always been the rejector. Playing the role of the rejected wasn't who I was or would ever be.

Finally, late one glorious night at my office, we found ourselves stumped on a case while eating cold Chinese food out of cartons. Somewhere between offering her the last eggroll and discovering the evidence I needed to win, we ended up doing it on my desk on top of a stack of legal briefs. How it commenced or who provoked the first move remains a blur. It wasn't exactly the most romantic way to begin a relationship, but after sleeping together we started dating.

From that point forward, we collaborated on tons of cases until the unceremonious split. Lately, whenever Ally employed Looking Glass Consultants, David showed up in place of Madison. Don't get me wrong. No ill will for the guy resided inside of me, but after I ended things with his sister, he wasn't exactly thrilled with me. I couldn't blame the guy either. If someone had done what I did to Madison to one of my sisters, I'd be pissed off as well. My interactions with not only David but with Richard and Donna as well had become tragically uncomfortable.

Truth be told though, the Langmores were the worst offenders of racial slander and classic stereotyping. To my face they acted nice, polite, and very hospitable. Behind my back, I was a lowlife louse. A greasy, shifty Italian who wasn't worthy of their daughter's attention.

How can I be *so* sure of this? Easy. Madison had invited me to join the Langmores for a family reunion over a Fourth of July long weekend. Going wasn't on the top of my to-do list, but it meant something to her, so I went along for the ride. The first night we were there, Richard and Donna were speaking with relatives on the front porch and rather loudly, might I add. The terms and words they used to describe their disdain and disgust over Madison spending time with a guy like me were unnecessarily harsh. They were gravely concerned I'd propose and she'd say yes. How would it look? Their only daughter would be married to someone in the Mafia. Promptly the next morning, I feigned a work emergency and left the Lake George area without Madison becoming bent. The combination of not feeling welcome and Madison's desire to become my wife had created the perfect storm.

On the flip side of the equation, my entire family—extended included, adored Madison. They went above and beyond to include her in all things Santino-related. Hell, my mother even referred to Madison as her daughter to her neighbors and friends. Reflecting on everything today, what Richard and Donna thought shouldn't have been a factor. I wasn't dating or sleeping with them. Furthermore, when the topic of engagement came up at the Santino dinner table, I should've opened a dialogue with Madison about it later that night instead of plotting my escape. If I'd considered any of these avenues, there was a strong chance she would've understood and given the advancement of our relationship some more time.

"Look me in the eyes and tell me Madison is happily in love with Doctor No Nuts," I challenged.

Noel Wasserman—also known as Doctor No Nuts exclusively by me—was a local kids' dentist who was weak of body and mind, and scared of his own damn shadow. He wasn't a bad-looking guy. He was blond over blue, had an average build, and was a business casual dresser with insanely white teeth—not that I ever checked him out. In theory, on paper, he'd make a good husband. He had an incredibly stable job and income, was a professional, owned his car and home outright, was well-groomed, and had a few bucks socked away in the bank, but I encompassed all that crap too. The only reason Jennifer set them up in the first place was because Noel was Ryan's partner in their dental practice. He'd been an available, easy target to kick me in the balls with. Nowhere in my brain did I imagine them lasting this long. Surely Madison would've grown tired of his mundane lifestyle, but she hadn't.

Whenever I'd see them around town, my stomach churned. The first time it happened, an odd sensation occurred. I couldn't put my finger on it, but later I realized it was jealousy—a sentiment I'd never worn. Others were always envious of me. The turn of events didn't sit well with me. It still doesn't. Madison was standing outside of a local bakery on Christmas Eve, sipping coffee and looking thoughtfully at a holiday window display. As I started to approach her, Doctor No Nuts came out of nowhere, and they kissed. A long, slow, passionate one. She beamed with joy while laughing lightly. The beast within me wanted to punch him, then grab her, and show her how a real man could make her feel. He didn't deserve someone as beautiful as Madison. Only *I* did. Her mess of unruly, mahogany curls, fierce, green eyes, tanned skin, and tight curves had my tongue dragging on the floor whenever she was nearby. Twig-like girls never turned me on. A female with some meat on their bones always did the trick. Madison's body was what I'd consider solid. Not skinny, but not obese. Toned and perfect. Just right. In and out of bed, her shape fit mine seamlessly. She belonged to me. Period. Case closed.

"It's none of your business, but yeah, she is. In fact, I'm meeting Noel on my lunch break to help him pick out an engagement ring." Jennifer's stance was firm and rather assertive. Her arms were ridged by her side, while her feet were planted shoulder length apart, and her back was ramrod straight. This posture revealed her words were truthful and direct.

Instantly, my heart dropped. Dating is one thing. Sure, it's a commitment, but not a serious one like marriage is. She couldn't say yes. If she did, I'd lose Madison forever. Screw that. Over my dead, rotting corpse would the Wasserman/Langmore union occur.

"If that's what she wants, a lifetime with dull Doctor No Nuts, then I'm happy for her," I said, attempting to not sound too pissed off.

"It's what *she* wants. Stay away from her, Luca," Jennifer warned.

"You got it, *Jenny*." Winking at her and producing the best Cheshire-Cat grin any scorned man could muster, the wheels inside of my brain started turning, carefully crafting a creative, but simple way to coincidently run into Madison when she was alone. Though Madison was a unique individual, her daily routine was rather predictable.

"Santino. My office, now. You can feel sorry for yourself on your own time," Ally ordered, appearing out of nowhere.

I was thrilled to have the last barbed word with Jennifer. Turning on my heel, my cool, easy, college boy swagger led me to Ally's space. Not only did my walk mask the rage monster roaring within my gut, but it also gave off an air of cocky confidence, which in this profession was a necessity.

"Is your head on straight or are you emotionally compromised over learning your ex is getting married?" she inquired.

"Madison Langmore is free to do whatever she'd like," I countered, casually stretching my back, then closing the door.

"We both know that's bullshit, Santino."

"Bullshit or not, it's irrelevant. Moving along. What do you need?" I guess it wasn't enough that Ally owned my ass for one hundred solid hours a week. The remaining sixty-eight were mine to do whatever I so desired, free of the firm's hold and control. What occurred outside of these walls was absolutely none of her damn business.

"Are you familiar with the names Nick and Jillian Winters?" Ally asked. She was already seated behind her massive, white, marble desk. She motioned for me to do the same across from her.

"Yeah. He's a shrink. He used to write self-help books and had a podcast, but now he cohosts a morning program with his wife, Jillian, who previously anchored

The Bottom Line. They were involved in a cult abduction thing a little while ago. It was broadcast all over social media. Everyone in the office stopped what they were doing to watch the live feed when the shit was going down. The wife shot two people—killed one, maimed the other, but she was never charged. Her lawyer finagled one of the most beautiful self-defense deals in the history of ever. I believe Charles Downey was the attorney on record, but don't quote me on that."

Wondering where this conversation was going, I prayed it wasn't going to lead to tons of additional new work. Currently, my office resembled the campsite of a homeless person. I hadn't seen the top of my desk in months due to mountains of papers, all which required my immediate attention. Don't get me started on the floor or filing cabinets. Even with associates' assistance, there were far too many cases to keep up with.

"That more or less sums it up." She leaned back in her chair. Her long, well-manicured fingernails clutched the armrests. Ally was one hell of a good-looking older broad with her tight, slender frame, mocha skin, and jet-black hair.

"What do you need me to do?" I asked, impatiently waiting for her to cut to the chase.

"The Winters were referred to us by Charles Downey—the original *finagler*. Doctor Winters believes he's being blackmailed by Sarah Davis—the woman Mrs. Winters accidentally shot in the foot. The extortionist suggests Sarah Davis's child, a son, is Doctor Winters's, and if he doesn't do what he's told, the story will go viral. He's admitted to sleeping with her without protection, not willingly, but rather under duress, meaning there's a possibility the child is his, but he's never seen the baby. The Winters have been paying to keep it out of the papers, but have decided they no longer wish to play the game. They're demanding a paternity test. If Doctor Winters is the father, he and Mrs. Winters want full custody of the child. Since Charles's firm doesn't handle cases of this nature, they're our problem now."

"They're on retainer?"

"As of this morning. Because they want this done as swiftly and quietly as possible, I contacted Donna from Looking Glass Consultants. Someone from their office will be here by noon. The information the Winters provided is comprehensive—emails, texts, letters, bank withdrawal slips for the blackmail money, but it's not enough to pin Ms. Davis to it. She never signed anything. Postmarks can't be traced. IP addresses bounce from country to country. Text messages come from random burner phones we can't ping, nor is there any public record of her having a baby, meaning there might not be one. All of the financial transfers go to an offshore shell corporation. She may or may not be working with a co-conspirator to ensure anonymity. I reached out to her a few minutes ago to introduce myself as the Winters' attorney and to inquire if she had legal representation I could get in touch with, but she hung up without answering the question. This might've spooked her, so she could be on the move. I need you to find as much as you can on her and the Winters. You're going to have to dig deep with this one, so move your ass. Coordinate with whoever shows up from Looking Glass—probably David because you pissed off Madison. This case takes top priority. Pause whatever you're working on. Any questions?" she asked, sliding a file across the desk's shiny surface. As she did this her thick, gold bracelets clanked against one another.

"How sure are we Sarah Davis has anything to do with this? Again, the shooting was all over social media and in the news for weeks. I understand the names of the victims were never posted or published for purposes of privacy, but their faces were visible on Jillian Winters's live feed. Undoubtedly someone recognized one of them. This could be a hoax. Somebody capitalizing on an innocent, mentally ill woman's name to score a quick buck from two very wealthy people. How many other individuals were abducted along with her? How many hospital workers were around Sarah? Maybe it's one of them? It's also possible Sarah shared intimate details of what happened with a new friend, neighbor, hell, even the kid who bags her groceries at the local market. This is a needle in a haystack case. Come on now, Ally." I leaned back in my chair, crossing my arms against my chest.

"You're right. We don't know who's involved or behind anything at this point. This could end up being a wild goose chase, but that's *your* job to find out, and I'm confident you will. Anything else?"

"Yeah, about a dozen time sensitive case files on my desk, seven of which are headed to deposition next week and three slated for trial by month's end. That's in addition to the heaping pile of other lawsuits I'm handling. How do you propose I juggle all of that?"

"Associates," she said rather matter-of-factly.

"They're morons."

"Then you're not training them properly."

An annoyed, blank expression served as my response.

"That look might make all the girls you socialize with drop their panties, but not this one. Go earn the seven figures I pay you, Santino."

"I'm on it," I said, leaving her space and going back to mine.

Awesome. There's nothing like starting your day off by finding out the woman you love is getting engaged to a man who's not you. Then, your boss decides you don't have enough work as it is, so she gifts you an impossible case. One sure to provide many hours of heartburn, headaches, and grief. The blackmailer could be anyone. How was I supposed to figure this out? Where the hell do I even begin?

An all too familiar right-eye stress trigger kicked up. The constant twitching could drive even the sanest of humans over the edge. Aggressively rubbing it away, I threw the folder Ally handed me on my desk. In a few hours David would waltz in. There was no way I'd give him the satisfaction of not having anything to show him. Especially because he'd open up his briefcase, and more than likely have the entire case solved. With a sigh and a huff, I sat. The first half of the morning was spent combing through paperwork, desperately trying to piece the ugly mess together. Best summed up? Somebody had it in for Nick Winters, but my gut suggested whoever was doing this wasn't working alone. They had to have help. Not even my father, a career criminal, could handle all of these angles at once without a support staff.

I decided Sarah Davis was the best and easiest place to begin. My fingers flew over the keyboard. I was frantic to find even a tiny scrap of something juicy before David arrived. At the moment, Sarah had no social media accounts, and the few online hits that popped up suggested she lived a simple, quiet life as an online homeschool teacher for a Catholic School. A small photograph placed beside her bio revealed a decent looking woman with shoulder-length, blonde hair, wide, brown eyes, and a slender face. Her last known place of residence was a small, neat home on the Nassau County-Queens border. There was no mention of children or a significant other. Just several dozen reviews mentioning her name on the school's webpage. According to them, parents and children loved her and her methods of educating. Softspoken, kind, gentle, understanding, and engaging were terms thrown around to describe Sarah.

Reclining in my chair, I tossed my reading glasses aside, and ran my hands through my beard. This case had all of the markings of a nightmare, and my life felt like an even bigger one. Usually, in situations like this, I knew or at least had an idea to run with about whom to point a finger at. Even if I'd been wrong, a new branch would grow leading me in another direction, and eventually to the person or persons responsible. This time? I hadn't a single frigging clue. There were too many players in the game. Aside from Nick and Jillian being celebrities, he came from the powerful, corrupt, political Winters family. Currently, his brother was attempting to get a party nomination to run for president. His sisters were both knee-deep in wars with the Senate and Congress, and his father was always pissing someone off by doing something shady as hell, Mr. Speaker of the House, Tag Winters. And you can't forget about Beau Winters, the head of this shifty family. He was largely loved by the people for his party line crossing while Vice President, but there was always a carefully concealed devious glint of evil in each expression he ever made. However, Sarah was the easy, convenient person to place blame upon—right now. Thousands of articles and reports were written after the abduction causing doubt to linger that the Winters family might've been involved in one way, shape, or form. How? Not a clue in the world, but my gut suggested they were worth a second glance. Tons of angry people, and not enough time to investigate them all.

Combine that with the knowledge Doctor No Nuts was about to propose to *my* girl, I'd never wanted a drink or cigarette as badly in my life—two nasty habits I kicked over a year ago because of Madison. I glanced at the clock on my desk. It read a little before noon. In a few minutes David would arrive, pompous attitude and all, making me feel like the biggest piece of shit failure to ever walk the face of the Earth.

"The second I break free from this prison, I'm buying a carton of Marlboros, a bottle of vodka, and getting hammered. Laid too. Twice. Screw that, three times, and once in the morning. I'm not going to make her breakfast either. She'll get a cup of coffee and a pat on the ass goodbye," I mumbled, scrolling through my contacts list in a desperate attempt to find a random woman to message. My eyes stopped on Madison's name. My index finger hovered above the link. I debated whether or not to reach out. Maybe I'd be able to convince her to grab a quick bite to eat. That would allow us to sit down and talk. If I got lucky enough, I might even be able to sway her to dump Doctor No Nuts and get back together with me.

"Yeah, okay. Nothing in life is ever easy. You should know that by now."

"You're absolutely right, but please don't start

smoking again. It's so gross and the woman you select to take to bed tonight and do four times will feel like she's making out with an ashtray," an all too familiar voice spoke. "But, to deprive her of your eggs en cocotte with bacon would be the real crime here."

My head snapped up. My tongue instantly tied. There she was. Beauty personified was standing in my office. Her emerald gem eyes were staring at mine. After months of not speaking, the first thing she overhears is me in my worst form confirming why she didn't need me in her life.

Look alive, jerkoff. Say something to recover.

But sadly, no words came out.

Chapter 2

Madison

"I'm sorry. Did I catch you at a bad time? I can come back later." Knowing Luca for as long as I had, his appearance, all of it, read off.

"What are you doing here?" Luca asked. It couldn't have been more obvious that he was stunned to see me standing in his personal space unannounced.

"Ally called. She said she needed assistance with a case. Has that changed?"

Please say it has because I have zero desire to be here, staring down the barrel of having to work with you. The nice girl act is a feat for short periods of time. Keeping it going for any longer than a few minutes could cause a vein in my head to rupture, especially after hearing you say that you're looking to get drunk and screwed tonight. Man, oh man, you dodged a bullet when he dumped you...

Yeah, okay. Keep telling yourself that. Maybe one day you'll believe it.

"No. Surprised to see you is all. You look fantastic. How have you been?" He answered with a slight smirk and a head tilt.

I had to look away or else the pain I'd worked so hard to shed would, beyond a shadow of a doubt return. There was no way that I'd permit him to bear witness to me tearing up. A carefree, balanced, happy, strong woman was all Luca was allowed to view. Giving him the power of knowing he'd wrecked my heart wasn't about to happen. Not today. Not ever.

We'd been broken up for quite some time, but truthfully, I never got over him. Luca Santino remained a weakness. Staying away from him and having my brother handle Newman and Associates LLP's caseload was easy. David, my fiercely protective older brother, immediately swapped one of his clients with mine so he'd be the one dealing with Ally's requests, while working side by side with Luca. The change of venue operated well until this morning when Ally called. David's wife, Tara, went into early labor, making me the only one available to get the details. My mother wasn't a private investigator; she managed the office, and my father was too busy juggling several of his own clients at once. With a heavy sigh and an epic eye roll, I reluctantly agreed.

After a year of exclusive dating, out of nowhere Luca ended the relationship. No explanation. He just showed up at my house after going MIA for a week saying it was over, using the classic, 'It's not you, it's me,' line of bullshit. As quickly as we started was as fast as we were done. In hindsight, I should've seen the writing on the wall. After his hasty exit while vacationing with my family at Lake George, my gut warned me the end was nigh, but my heart didn't want to believe he'd lie about an emergency work thing randomly popping up. Hey, it could happen, right? Ally Newman had a reputation for being a slave driver, demanding her employees were always on call, day or night. Aside from Jennifer Glick, Luca was her other go-to person making the story feasible.

However, another warning occurred a few weeks prior when we were at his family's house for dinner. Every Wednesday and Sunday the Santinos gathered for a meal that could feed the entire United States Armed Forces and then some. That particular night, somewhere between Gina Santino serving the pasta and dessert courses, the topic of marriage came up. His mother kept pressing the matter, endlessly inquiring if I wanted to be a wife and a mother. To get her to stop, I answered by telling her that I did and do, but it didn't seem like it was in the cards right then and there.

Silence filled the car on the ride back to my home. Luca wore an expression caught somewhere between wanting to vomit and run away, never to return. I won't lie. It hurt, bothered, upset, and angered me. After being together for a year if he had no intention of moving forward, what was the point? My heart sank, feeling used and taken advantage of. I was good enough to date and sleep with, but not marry? Usually he'd stay over, but that night he dropped me off and hauled ass off of the block. His metallic blue Camaro ZL1 left tire marks on the asphalt—true story. They're still there if you'd like to see them for yourself. An internal debate consumed me for days over whether I should or shouldn't explain my response to his mother, but anything said would've been a lie. I did want to get married and have children, and I did want that with him.

A few days after the break-up while having drinks at a local bar with Jennifer, drowning my sorrows in bottomless mojitos, Luca approached our table. The bragging bastard wanted to know if we'd like for him and his date to leave to spare my feelings. I'd never wanted to throat punch someone as much as I did right then and there. Of course, I lied my ass off and played the role of the easy-breezy, it's all good ex-girlfriend. Upon arriving home, I crawled under the covers and prayed for death because my heart felt as if it were tearing in two. All I could focus on was him and the trampy blonde he'd been with doing it. For weeks I didn't leave the house. My brain couldn't stop reeling, which meant no work was done or positive distractions were had. Just Luca swimming around in my every waking and non-waking thought. If it wasn't for Jennifer, I'd still be in hiding, wallowing in self-pity with a carton of ice cream in hand. I really thought Luca and I were end-game material. Apparently, we were not. In true best friend form, Jennifer forced me to rejoin the human race, got me back on my feet, and introduced me to Doctor Noel Wasserman, never once uttering the phrase, "I told you so," even though she knew from the get-go Luca would dismiss me, leaving me high and dry.

Noel is a great guy. The town loves him. His calm, gentle, understanding nature quickly earned him a solid place in the pediatric dental community. He never yelled or ignored me. If anything, the man worshiped the ground I walked on, making sure my every need or want was met, immediately, if not sooner. Noel checked off all of the boxes I was looking for in a husband, except one. He wasn't Luca, who incidentally checked off none of the boxes. Luca was wild, reckless, impatient, adventurous, charming, and drop-dead gorgeous. Noel is the polar opposite. That's not to say Noel wasn't attractive, because he is. He's simply not built like Luca with washboard abs, tremendous arms, and an ass that went on for days. In spite of Luca being absolutely wrong for me, he'd become a drug of sorts. The combination of his thick, spiked black hair, brown eyes that always hinted at mischief, olive complexion, a killer smile hidden beneath a cropped beard, and a body straight out of a men's fitness magazine, slew me. His flirtatious charisma and heavy New York accent were murderous. Besides the physical attraction, Luca was a beyond brilliant attorney. That man knew the law inside and out. Hell, who am I kidding? He knew me inside and out too.

Don't forget about his commitment issues and the fact that he's a male whore. He had quite the womanizing reputation before dating you. Never once did you treat him poorly. He pissed on you, not the other way around. If he loved you, he never would've thrown you away, nor would he have been scared to propose. Luca Santino played your ass and you fell for it hook, line, and sinker. He stole one year of your life that you'll never get back. Grin. Play nice in the sandbox. Wrap this assignment up as fast as possible and walk away. David will take the next case, and Luca can go back to being rearview mirror material. Just don't let him see the scar he left. The one you frequently pick at, refusing to allow it to heal.

On top of forcing radiance that caused an internal pain so deep I thought my ribs might crack, I wrestled with the injured little girl inside of me who wanted to flee, hide, and cry over how much my soul still craved and missed him.

"Great. Thanks. David would've been here to handle this, but Tara's having the baby, so you're stuck with me. Ally already provided preliminary details. This won't be a cakewalk, but I'm confident if there's anything to uncover, we will. I'll email you my findings in a few days. We can touch base and compare notes. Suspect-wise this is an epic mess, but my gut says it's not an outsider doing this. It's Sarah Davis or someone attached to her. I don't know why I feel this way, but I do. I plan to start with her and work my way out if she's a dud. Good?" I asked, desperate to take off.

"Yeah, sure. If that's what you want. In the past, we never worked a case like that, though. We always examined all angles and avenues together. Even when David or Richard is here, that's how we do it, but if this setup is better for you, then by all means. Please send my sincerest congratulations to your family. Since you want to cover the Sarah Davis angle, I'll work my end a little differently. This way we'll cover more ground quicker. If possible, I'd like the names and whatever other information you can come up with of all of the abductees who were held with Davis. I also request a list of hospital personnel—doctors, nurses, and so on who treated her." Luca's tone denoted traces of being taken aback. He wasn't lying. Historically, we did work jobs side by side, but I couldn't any longer. Being around him weighed too heavily on my head and heart. The handful of moments together now had caused an ache so deep, pressure in my chest had formed making breathing difficult. If I couldn't get past my personal issues with Luca, I wouldn't be able to give this assignment one hundred percent of my attention. My parents invested their lives and livelihood in Looking Glass Consultants. To screw up a job over hurt feelings would not only let them down, but would tarnish the company's stellar reputation. I glanced quickly in his direction. The boyish smirk he once sported had vanished.

"This new way is better. I'll see what I can dig up,"

I said, still clinging to fake expressions with such ferocity my jaw hurt.

"Again, if that's what you want." He reclined in his chair, crossing his massive biceps over his chiseled chest.

"Great. Thanks. We'll be in touch," I said, turning around, ready to bolt.

"Doesn't mean we can't grab lunch," Luca added, stopping me dead in my tracks.

"Another time."

"What's wrong with today?" he challenged, reaching for and putting his reading glasses on.

"I should get up to the hospital to check on Tara." It wasn't exactly a total lie. I had planned on swinging by, just not right then.

"For what? To assist the doctor in the delivery process? To sit in the waiting room reading magazines from the Truman administration? They'll call when the baby arrives and they're situated in a room, ready for visitors. Been there. Done that many times with my sisters. Come on. Let's go get something to eat at Enzo's."

"Enzo's is forty-five minutes away—and that's without traffic."

"So? Is it not your favorite place to get pizza anymore?"

"We're *really* going to do this, huh?" I wished my tone revealed a firmer stance than the weakness I clearly heard bleeding through.

"Do what, Mads?" he inquired, leaning forward, and cocking an eyebrow.

The sound of him referring to me by the nickname he created, one I *never* allowed others to use because I hated it, made my knees weaken. Whenever Mads came out of his mouth, I always melted.

"We're colleagues and acquaintances, *not* friends. I'd prefer you view this interaction in that fashion *only*, and furthermore, it's respectfully requested I be referred to as Ms. Langmore, *not* Mads. Thank you." The resolve I sought had finally found its voice. A sense of strength filled my core.

"First of all, I'm always a consummate professional. No need for concern there. Second, you're right. We're *not* friends. We're former *intimate* partners. Now, I can handle that, but I'm unsure you can, *Ms. Langmore*." His tone darkened.

"Consummate narcissist is more fitting," I mumbled, unable to stop the words from coming out of my mouth.

"Excuse me?" He stood.

"You know what? You're right, *but* it's not that I can't handle this. I don't want to be around you. Ally can hire someone else. Let them deal with the almighty Luca Santino. A man with no regard for anyone except himself. You're a cruel, nasty, arrogant, womanizing, lying, manipulating, douchebag of a human. Being here talking to you as if nothing's the matter makes my stomach turn. I can't stand you, and I will never forgive you for what you did to me. How you wasted my time. How you preyed on my love when all the while you never gave a damn about me." Abandoning a paying job to get away from him was well worth it. My father would understand. I'd spin some bullshit story to Ally to insure she'd call upon our services again, and leave, never to return. However, speaking my truths felt empowering.

Luca sighed heavily—his classic telltale sign of

frustration. "I get it. You're angry and upset, which I deserve. I wish you would've chewed my ass out last year, but nevertheless, here we are. Please, speak your mind. Get it all off of your chest. Say whatever you've got to say. Unburden the soul. I can take it. When you're through, we can start working on the case with a clean, *professional* slate."

I arched forward and planted my palms flat against the very same wooden desk we'd made love on for the first time. Our eyes locked. "You're not worth my while or energy. Got news for you—you never were," I hissed. In that fleeting moment, a sexual heat, a tension so powerful exploded inside of my core causing self-control and sound-mind decision-making skills to fight like hell to remain in a governing state.

"Oh, *Vita Mia*. If that were the truth, you wouldn't be standing here fighting with me. This is *exactly* where you want to be and I'm *exactly* who you desire to be with. If it still hurts, you still care. Now that we've settled that, let me know when you find something we can give to Ally. My cell number is the same. I'm sure you still have it memorized. Talk then," Luca challenged. His spot-on perception irritated me.

"You don't get to call the shots anymore, *babe*," I seethed.

"Maybe I don't. Who knows? Who really cares? But for the record, my love for you was never a manipulation or a lie, and it never will be. I still love you, *Ms. Langmore*. I loved you the moment I met you. Hell, I even loved you right here on this very desk." His tone and expression were dead serious.

"How dare you!" Without waiting for him to respond, I booked it out of the building, but not before slamming his office door shut with the force of one hundred men. Usually, I'd swing by Jennifer's office, but if I stayed for one more minute, I'd have either torn Luca's clothing off and done him on his cluttered workspace, or I would've ripped his heart out, so he'd feel how I did when he brusquely trashed me. Either way, I lost. The thrill of telling him off caused a spark of lust to ignite within me. His admission of still loving me created a spur of satisfaction. Good. He should. However, creating a sizable distance between us was quite necessary. Once I was on the street, safely away from Luca Santino, my cell phone rang.

"Langmore. What?" I hissed into the device.

"What did *he* do and say this time?" Jennifer asked.

"What makes you ask that?"

"Well, for starters, a few seconds ago I watched you storm out of here like you were on fire. Additionally, you smashed his door so hard the entire building shook. On top of that, you didn't swing by my office to see me. And lastly, you answered the phone like a savage. Dish. What happened? Want me to knee him in the balls for you?"

An unexpected laugh found its way out of my mouth. Truth be told, if I'd requested she kick Luca in the nuts, she would've, and happily. We met years ago as undergraduates after being assigned lab partners in a criminology class. Jennifer's hard-as-ice and rather standoffish demeanor never bothered me much. She was a workaholic and spent most of her free time obsessing over grades, but a part of her wanted to let loose. I helped bring that side out. When the semester ended, we had become best friends, even sharing an off-campus apartment the following term. Since then, our friendship grew into what it is today. Rain or shine, highs or lows, ups or downs, Jennifer Glick would always be there. "You know I love you most and best, right?"

"Yeah, yeah. Save the sweet talk for Noel."

"Are you working on anything major right now?" I asked.

"I'm always working on something major. Why? What's up?" I could hear the scratch and scraping of things roughly moving around her desk.

"When I wrap this case up for you guys, if you're free, I thought it might be nice to take a long girls' spa weekend at that place we went to a few years ago in Connecticut. Just you and me. No Ryan. No Noel."

"Oh, my God, yes. Please. Book it. I'm there." She sighed heavily. "Shit. Got to go. I have a lunch appointment I cannot be late for. Let me know if you change your mind about me causing massive amounts of physical pain to your asshole ex. Call me later?"

"Will do. Enjoy your lunch thing," I said, hanging up. Her call was exactly what I needed to calm the hell down from my encounter with Luca.

Deciding to forgo returning to my office, I went home for some peace and quiet—maybe a glass of wine too. I required space to sort through my emotions and to restore my lost inner balance. Laptop open, I sat at the dining-room table with a tumbler full of merlot, as the Winters file taunted me. *You can feel sorry for yourself later. Right now, there's a puzzle to solve, and no one figures out complicated better than you.*

Giving in to my natural curiosity—Ally had only provided the basics—I used my thumb and index finger to flip the folder open. Two hours later, engrossed in a way I'd never been before, I found myself reviewing the widely circulated video of Jillian Winters finding and saving her husband. This brave, fierce woman turned helplessness into power, going from villain to victor. As the court of public opinion pointed fingers, accusing her of committing this heinous act of potentially murdering her spouse, then stashing the body somewhere, I couldn't fathom what was going on inside of Jillian's head, or how she even found the strength to rescue Nick.

Could you ever do that? Stand tall in the face of adversity? Go to extremes and shoot someone for the man you loved?

Three reams of paper and an ink cartridge later, everything I'd found had been printed, sorted, and was ready for intense examination. Initially, nothing jumped off of the pages. This wasn't concerning. After well over a decade of being a private investigator, it happened from time to time. All it meant was I'd have to do a deeper dive. Glancing at the names I had jotted down in a notebook, my eyes kept zeroing in on Sarah Davis. Perhaps it was because my gut kept screaming that her hands were all over this. She'd allegedly started all of this drama, so why not look into her first? Granted, no solid evidence for an open-and-shut accusation presented itself, but that didn't mean squat. Sarah had simply placed some time and effort into covering her tracks. One of the first things I'd learned on the job was to never put anything past anyone, ever. People were capable of doing all sorts of weird, crazy crap for reasons one would never fully comprehend. Trust me, I've seen it all. Inputting her last known address into my cell phone GPS, I took off, praying this wasn't an empty lead. The sooner this case wrapped, the better. I'd be able to return to a blissful state of comfort with Noel, and Luca could go straight back to Hell, where he belonged.

Chapter 3

Luca

After a fourteen-hour day, I finally made it home. Shedding the monkey suit and the necktie noose, I showered, grabbed a bottle of beer from the fridge, and flipped on the Yankees game. My body sank into the couch. Attempting to erase the world around me was useless. My damn brain couldn't stop focusing on Madison. The fire in those jeweled eyes, the glint of lust while attempting to chew me out, the nice girl veil dropping to reveal her feisty side—a major turn-on. Doubt over her still caring about me vanished. If she'd gotten over us, she wouldn't have become nasty, and never would've appeared hot and bothered the closer our bodies drew. The kill shot? When I professed to still loving her, her body language clearly revealed delight. She'd work the case. There was no way Madison would walk away from it. I'd bet my life she went home, poured herself a chilled glass of red wine, opened the Winters file, and instantly became intrigued. In a few days, my phone would ring and it would be her all excited over something she found. When that happened, we'd meet up and I'd take the bull by the horns. By the time this was over, Doctor No Nuts would be a thing of the past because Madison, with my nudging, would remember how perfect we were together on all levels.

You hope.

Nope. I know.

While fiddling with my cell phone, my contemplation to reach out to Madison was quickly struck down by sound thinking and logic. Let Madison stew. Make her crave being in my company again. Stack the deck in my favor this time. Closing my eyes so I could fantasize about Madison on all levels felt beyond amazing, but unfortunately the blast of my ringing cell phone startled my ass back to reality. Assuming it was my mother's nightly check-in call, I clicked accept without paying attention to what was on the screen.

"Hey, Ma. What's going on?" I answered.

"Whatever or whomever you're screwing, stop. Meet me at the Gold Coast Diner now. Please," a woman's voice said hurriedly.

"Mads?" I sat up straighter.

Nothing. The line went dead.

Looking at the screen, I read '*Vita Mia,*' positively confirming it was, in fact, her. Jumping up, not caring that I had baggy gray sweats and a wife-beater style tank top on, I grabbed the black hoodie hanging by the door and my keys. Sprinting to my Camaro, I sped to the diner. My thoughts raced from one extreme to the next. Why would Madison reach out to me, someone she suggested she couldn't stand several hours ago, if she found herself in trouble? Calling Richard, Donna, Noel, Jennifer, or David made more sense. Spotting her parked, black Suburban, I scaled the steps to the restaurant three by three. She stood in the lobby, waiting. Her nails drummed against the back of the plastic cell phone case she held onto. A certain air of nervous energy surrounded her entire being. How could I tell? I knew her and *all* of her tells, well.

"Are you okay, Mads?" I questioned. My voice was imbibed with concern. Without asking her permission, I ran my hands up and down her arms, inspecting her for any injuries. Physically, she appeared well.

"How many?" A hostess interrupted.

"Two. A booth in the back, please," I said. My full attention immediately returned to Madison. The fact she allowed my fingers to linger on her body was a good, and a bad, sign. Nothing out of the ordinary presented, and there was no visible blood, but after this morning's spat, the only reason she'd allow me to continue to touch her was if she required comfort unattainable from anyone else in the universe.

"What's with the cloak-and-dagger act, Mads? You almost gave me a damn heart attack thinking you were in trouble or hurt," I asked, once we were seated.

"Look at this." She handed me a tablet from her oversized purse. The picture app was open.

Glancing at the first photo, I saw a young woman with shoulder-length, blonde hair getting out of a small, dark blue, cheap, compact car. Several consecutive shots revealed her walking into a house. Scrolling through the remaining images, close-ups of the vehicle showed the license plate, a rear-facing car seat secured behind the passenger's side, and a silhouette of two people—the woman and a masculine figure, through curtains on the second floor of the home. My left index finger kept swiping right until a selfie of Madison and Noel appeared. Doctor No Nuts was kissing her cheek while she smiled brightly. Dropping the device on the table with a huff and eye roll, I regretted the action instantly. I wasn't in the mood to go another round with her today.

"I didn't break us, Luca. *You* did. You have no right

to get pissed off that I moved on," she snapped, inspecting the table for any damage.

"Did you run the plate?" I inquired, refusing to respond to the jab. Now wasn't the time or the place.

"Yeah. I had my father do it. The car is registered to Noah Lessor, Warren Lessor's cousin. He was involved with the Nick Winters abduction. Noah was kept in a treatment facility for about seven months post the incident, then he was discharged to outpatient services, which he still attends bi-weekly via telephone. The house is solely in Sarah Davis's name, but after watching the property today and after snooping through surface trash in the pails that were on the curb of the property, I realized Noah receives mail there. His driver's license is linked to that address as well."

"So, what do you need or want me to do? Sounds like you have something to give Ally," I said in an uncaring tone. Even though she'd produced quality evidence, the image of Noel's lips touching any part of Madison angered me deeply.

"Well, first, drop the attitude or this isn't going to work. Second, some help with finding more information on Lessor and Davis's health records would be great."

"No attitude here. However, hacking into medical records is illegal. Find some DNA samples when you go dumpster diving again—for the baby too. Have Metrix Data run whatever you can collect, then give me the results and the bill. I can work with that, *legally*. Even a dirty diaper will do the trick. Ally says there's no record of Davis giving birth, but that doesn't mean anything. She could've had the baby at home and never declared it to the state, or perhaps she gave birth under a different name. She wouldn't be the first woman to fudge a birth certificate. Generally speaking, since people don't drive around with car seats when they're childless, all roads lead to her or him having a small kid. Is that all?"

"Looking Glass has always conducted investigations on the up and up. Your suggestion that I'd ask you, an officer of the court, to do something illegal is insulting," she scoffed.

"My apologies. I must've misunderstood what you were asking for," I countered, glancing at my watch.

This impromptu meeting wasn't going well. Maybe if I hadn't shown noticeable signs of annoyance over the picture it might've, but how does one control a visceral reaction? You can't. You don't. At this juncture there was no chance of recovering from it because neither she nor I appeared to be in the proper frame of mind to deal with the other. But butt-hurt emotions will do that to you.

"Got a hot date keeping your bed warm at home?" she snapped.

"Guess *Doctor No Nuts* is busy tonight? Perhaps his lunch date with Jenny to find the perfect engagement ring for you ran a little later than expected?" I shot back, immediately cringing. I'd spilled the beans about what Jennifer shared in private. Jealousy had gotten the better of me. "You weren't supposed to know that. I'm sorry. Strike my last statement from the record."

"What?" she asked in disbelief.

"Nothing. Nothing. Seriously, forget what I said. I was talking out of my ass. Great, the waitress is here. She'll have a bacon cheeseburger, with tomato, extra well done. I'll have a gyro. We'd like a side of mozzarella fries with gravy, and a French onion soup with two spoons, please." We'd been to this particular diner tons of times. Remembering what she liked and disliked hadn't faded from my memory.

"Anything to drink?"

"A Diet Coke with lime, and a seltzer with lemon. Thank you."

"You got it, hon," the waitress said, leaving us alone again.

"He's going to propose?" Madison practically shouted. She appeared confused and totally freaked out over this newfound information.

"Shhh," I whispered, frantically leaning across the table in a feeble attempt to erase the past five minutes by containing her wildly waving hands.

Her breathing became short and her eyes widened. She appeared as if she was on the verge of a panic attack. Sliding beside her, I placed an arm around her shoulder, and pulled her close.

"That was supposed to be a secret. Jennifer said it this morning to piss me off. I'm so sorry, Mads, but hey. It might not even be true. As I said, the comment was meant to annoy me."

Tucking her rigid frame deeper into my side, I felt her warm breath tease my neck. Plain and simple, it was pure torture.

"Isn't this what you wanted? Marriage? Kids? Do you not want to be Noel's wife?" I inquired, no longer cursing myself and my big, fat mouth. Her reaction spoke volumes, which worked in my favor.

"I have to get out of here," she said, pushing me out of the booth.

"Where are you going to go? Home? No one's there. To your parents' house? Guess what? They'll probably be over the moon Doctor No Nuts wants to marry their baby girl, grateful it's not the no good, mobbed-up,

Guinea who'll never be worthy enough for the Langmores. Jennifer feels that way too. Who's left? David and Tara? They're kind of busy with the new baby at the moment. Noel? He's the one you appear to be running from. So, the way I see it is stay. Enjoy a meal with and talk to your loser ex-boyfriend," I said.

Sitting ramrod straight, she inhaled and exhaled deeply for several long moments before speaking again.

"After we finish up here, I'll go back to Davis's house. It'll be late. Hopefully, everyone in the home will be asleep and won't see or hear me snooping around outside. The trash cans are on the curb. Tomorrow is garbage day. If a child is involved, I'm sure there will be a mountain of dirty diapers in at least one of the cans. As for compiling a list of the other abductees and hospital workers involved in this mess, I request we explore and exhaust this avenue before branching out. It's just a hunch, but I'm confident Davis is behind this and not someone else looking to cash in on her tragedy. I watched Jillian Winters's video again. Davis was noticeably angry and upset with Nick Winters for tricking her into believing he loved her. Normally, when a woman has been hurt by a significant other, she wallows, cries, curses him out, plots ways to get him back, or wounds him in a similar fashion by moving on. However, Davis isn't playing with a full deck. When an emotionally imbalanced female becomes irritated—well, Hell hath no fury. I need you to be patient while I perform my investigation. Please." She paused. "Before you ask, I'm not mad at you for letting the cat out of the bag, so don't waste your breath asking. And, if you apologize one more time, I'll throat-punch you. I know how to. You taught me. Remember? Let's be honest—

you're not sorry and that's okay."

"Let me go with you for old times' sake," I said, not wanting her to be alone tonight.

"Sounds like a plan." She produced the fakest of smiles. "Great. Our food is here. The cheese on top of that soup is mine—just letting you know. You can have the soggy, sour bread inside."

"Whatever you'd like, *Ms. Langmore.*" I winked.

"I like it better when you call me Mads or *Vita Mia.*" She shrugged and proceeded to cut her burger and my gyro in half, placing one side on each plate.

"I can live with that." I allowed comfort from the past to seep into the moment, soaking it up because it wouldn't last long. Eventually, reality would catch up. It always did.

Chapter 4

Madison

"Okay, so she obviously has a baby, or six million," Luca whispered, as we nosed through one of Davis's garbage pails. "There's like a billion diapers in here. How many craps can one tiny human take in a twenty-four-hour period? Better question—what the hell is she feeding it?"

"Grab a few and toss them in the bag. I'm elbow-deep in Chinese food takeout containers that stink like they expired last year," I said.

"Want to trade?" he quipped.

"Yeah, no, thanks," I said, tying the sack I'd been working with shut, and praying that would contain the stench. "All done?"

"Yes, ma'am. Let's go," he said, seizing our finds. "Hopefully, we collected enough DNA and various other evidence so we don't have to do this again."

"Please. You know you love reeking like a dumpster," I joked.

"Uh, yeah. Of course. Who doesn't? It's such a turn-on."

A pang of longing snapped at my heart. I missed our sarcastic banter. Noel didn't engage in behavior like that. Whenever I'd let a droll statement fly out of my mouth, I'd be treated to a kind, gentle reminder that sarcasm was the lowest form of wit, and I was better than that crude, crass, classless behavioral style.

Once we were back on the main road, I couldn't stop a repressed bout of laughter from exiting my mouth. It'd been forever since Luca and I acted as partners in crime. It felt amazing. Like a blindfold had been removed and I could see again. That was the thing about Luca. He made you feel *all* of the things, not just some, unlike Noel. I was free to be me—every last ounce. The good, bad, and indifferent.

"What's so funny?"

"In your craziest dreams did you ever imagine you'd be digging through mountains of trash just to earn a living as a lawyer?"

"Absolutely. Right after pleading cases before the Supreme Court Justices."

"Stick with me, babe. I'll take you to all of the elegant places and show you the finer things in life." Unexpectedly, my hand reached for and rested on top of his right knee. Upon realizing what I'd done, what happened next remained a mystery. Did I leave it and see how he'd respond? Or, should I move it, pretending like it never happened?

"As long as you're there, you can take me anywhere and show me anything you'd like, *Vita Mia*. We make a good team," he said. His thick, strong fingers wove into mine. His dark, mischievous eyes never left the road.

"We really do."

"Tomorrow, I'll run shit bag number one up to the lab and have them put a rush on it. I should have the results back quickly. With Lessor and Davis already in the system because of the abduction, matching DNA against them shouldn't be too difficult. While we wait, we can dig through shit bag number two. By week's end this might be wrapped up," Luca said.

"Yeah." An involuntary sigh slid out of my mouth. Reality hit, and hard. Not only did I have to deal with Noel proposing and unresolved feelings for Luca, but now what the future held. What would happen when this case came to a close? I loved Noel. He was a good man. Smart, attractive, settled, cared tremendously for me, present, and loyal, always putting me and my needs first, but did I want to spend forever with him? Was I ready to settle for a love that didn't feel as strong as it had with another man? However, even the blind could've seen this coming. We'd been dating for a long time, but I never put much stock in it actually happening mainly because we never talked about it for longer than a few minutes. We both wanted to get married, have kids, get a dog, and live the American dream, but that's as far as we had gotten. There'd been no discussion of moving in together or anything like that. At times we'd spend the night at the other's house, but it wasn't a permanent setup. Nothing of his had ever been left at my home and vice versa. Leaning back in the seat and closing my eyes for a fleeting second, I imagined the best-case scenario for that moment. If I could have anything at this very minute, what would it be? Who'd be driving the car? Where would we be going? Doing? Coming from?

I could lie and say I saw Noel and we were heading home with a few kids in the backseat all sleeping, tired from our day out at some amusement park or the beach, but that wasn't the case. What I did see was Luca and me going back to our place.

"You don't have to decide tonight what you're going to tell Noel when he pops the question. Wait for the big event. Go with your gut when the situation comes around," Luca said, breaking the silence.

"When did you become a mind reader?" A certain amount of comfort was felt over how well Luca understood me and my moods.

"I know you, Mads. I'm familiar with all of your expressions. The one you're sporting is a lost in a deep thought one. It's not a race to get to the altar or to parenthood. Just because you feel you've reached a certain age where it's expected you get married and start a family doesn't mean you have to."

"You're right." I smiled, not wishing to discuss this any further.

"I'm *always* right, *Vita Mia*," he joked.

The sound of his easy laugh caused a stirring deep within me. Now, I'm aware my next move was a classic shady one, but don't judge a girl until you've walked in her shoes. After Luca dropped me back at the diner and we said goodnight by exchanging a rather awkward embrace, I may have deliberately left my cell phone on the passenger seat. He'd see it for sure and would have to swing by my house to return it because he'd have no other way to call or text me, and he knew I lived and died by my electronics. I don't know why I did it. A moment of insanity. A need for an escape. An act of missing him so much it hurt every bone in my body, and seeing him made that ache worse. Not a clue, but here we were. The plan seemed flawless.

By the time I pulled into my driveway, he wasn't there. An hour passed, providing plenty of time for me to shower and change into more alluring night attire, but still nothing. Sitting at the dining room table attempting to work was impossible. As I closed my laptop lid getting ready to call it a day, a knock echoed throughout my house.

"Okay. You got me back here, but I have no idea why. Care to explain?" Luca said softly, leaning against the door frame. His right hand held my phone while his left toyed with his beard.

"I think you already know the answer to that particular question."

"No, I don't believe I do. Why don't you tell me?"

"I'd much rather show you," I flirted.

"Are you sure that's a good idea?" A glint of hesitation resided inside of each word.

"I've never been as sure of something in my entire life," I whispered, pulling him by the front of his sweatshirt into the house and slamming the door shut.

Chapter 5

Luca

Slowly, my eyes opened. Initially, the space around me made no sense. It took a hot second for the events of last night to rise to the surface. After spotting Madison's phone in my car, I knew immediately she'd left it behind on purpose. That girl clung to it—her tablet and laptop too, never letting them out of her sight. But why recklessly abandon such a valuable item? What was the motive? The desired result? For the next few hours, an internal debate raged over returning it tonight or waiting until the morning. Perhaps it *was* an honest mistake? Surely by now, she realized the phone was missing. Madison encompassed a brilliant mind with a keen eye for even the tiniest of details. She'd had to have deduced it was at the diner, somewhere outside of the Davis house, or in my possession. Feasibly, an investigation had already began. Would she eventually show up at my door? Could it be she was playing a game of cat and mouse, trying to draw me out to see how far I'd go to win her back?

Determined for answers, I shoved my nerves aside and got my ass got back into my Camaro. Once I parked the car, trepidation caused me to take pause, making me hang back in the car reminding myself this might not be an act of Madison wanting me, and to not get my hopes up. However, after a brief flirtation, she attacked me like a lioness in heat, crushing her full, soft lips to mine. It shouldn't have happened. Madison was with Noel, but who the hell was I to deprive myself of something I'd been craving? Tomorrow we'd sort through the drama. What sucked was today was tomorrow—time to pay the piper.

Madison wasn't in bed when I rolled over, but the memory of what happened hours ago remained. Straining my ears for a clue as to where she was, I heard running shower water gently fill the emptiness. An old school twin bell clock on the nightstand alerted me that it was fairly early. My back slid up against the padded headboard, while my shoulders reclined. My brain was thrown into overdrive, desperately attempting to find a way to justify our actions to Madison in order to shield her from the moral quandary she more than likely resided in. A split-second decision was made to get up and shower in the guest bathroom down the hall. Always keeping a spare suit and a toiletry bag in my car, I went out, got it, and proceeded to get the day rolling. Once I finished, Madison greeted me in the kitchen with a kiss and a cup of coffee in hand.

"How'd you sleep, babe?" she asked. Her back was turned. Her attention was locked on whatever she had on the stove.

"Good. You?" I said, treading lightly, unsure of where this conversation would lead.

"Like the dead. I haven't slept that well in a long time. After you wrap up at the lab today, why don't you come back here? We can sort through the other bag of crap we picked up last night. I already told my parents I'd be working from home for the rest of the week since Ally wants this done as soon as possible. We both know when things are handled remotely I tend to be more productive. No office distractions. You know?" she suggested casually.

"Yeah. I remember. You're more than welcome to come to the lab with me," I offered, leaning against the counter beside the oven. The situation appeared off. Madison should've been freaking the hell out that she cheated on her boyfriend with her ex, but no. She came across as calm, almost happy. Like nothing out of the ordinary ever went down. The moment resembled old times.

"That's a great idea. The lab is near Davis's house. We can swing by afterwards and snoop a little more. See if we can snag a few pictures of Noah, or whoever the mystery man is. Maybe we can catch a glimpse of the baby too." Her tone was rather matter-of-fact.

What the hell? Is it possible she forgot we spent the night making love? Or worse, maybe she actively wants to erase it from her memory? Was it that bad? Was I that bad? But, then why call me babe and kiss me? Oh, man. I pray this doesn't become a thing where I have to talk her off of a ledge.

"Okay. Let me call Ally to tell her I'll be out of the office today." Not waiting for her to reply, a response could only make Madison change her mind, I headed outside to the front porch.

"Tell me you have something good, Santino," Ally said the second she answered.

"How about I tell you I have something great?"

"I'm intrigued."

"Knew you would be. Last night Madison found out Noah Lessor gets mail at the house on file for Sarah Davis. He was a part of the Nick Winters abduction case, *and* he's Warren Lessor's cousin. Madison took a ton of pictures of the house, the car Davis drives, which is registered to Lessor and has a baby seat inside of it. We also dug through a bunch of trash and found some noteworthy items I'll be running to the lab for DNA testing today. You don't, by chance, have any DNA samples from Nick Winters? I've got a few dirty diapers I'd like for the lab to study against his genetic material. If it comes back a match, there's your case."

"I don't, but I will call him the moment we finish speaking. I'll have Doctor Winters meet you at the lab and someone there can collect it. You'll be using Metrix Data on Elm in Floral Park?"

"Yes. I should be there around eleven. Tell him to meet me in the waiting room. Also, I'll be working remotely today, if that's possible. I want to help Madison go through what we unearthed last night so we can investigate it thoroughly and follow wherever it takes us. Track any leads. Plus, she wants to return to Davis's house to see if she can get eyes on Lessor. Ally, I read his file—he's a whack job. She shouldn't be going it alone. God forbid either of them sees her and flips out; it could end badly."

"Take all of the time necessary. I'll have some of the associates pull files from your desk and work on them. They'll also take care of your depositions and upcoming court appearances. Lighten your load a bit. Don't worry. You'll get all of the credit. Make sure to expense the lab fees and don't forget to clock last night's time for billables. Let me know if you need anything else."

"Of course. Thank you."

"You're working really hard to get that girl back. Don't blow it this time, Santino," she quipped before hanging up.

Inside of the house, Madison had set the table for two. She sat, waiting for me to join her. Doing so, I felt the necessary urge to address the elephant in the room.

"Are we forgetting about what happened last night?" I inquired. My head lowered. I couldn't bear to look her in the eyes out of fear she was about to tell me to get lost.

"Do you *want* to forget about it?" she countered.

The desire to look at her and to have her see my unspoken sentiments choked me, but my neck wouldn't budge. "I don't want to play games, Mads. You're with someone. I'm *not* okay being a side piece. I have feelings too."

"Who's playing games, Luca? Did you not enjoy what we did? Was it not what you wanted? Because if that's the case, you always had the right to say stop and I would've listened. But, if my memory serves correct, you appeared into it. I don't recall having to hold you down and force you into doing something you weren't willing to do. If anything, once we were in bed, you took the lead. Additionally, counselor, why did we go two rounds if you felt it was wrong? Why subject yourself to behaviors that don't support your moral narrative? Or, were you simply horny and I was a warm body to satisfy a need? What you said in your office yesterday about still being in love with me, was it not true?" Her arms folded tightly across her chest while her legs locked at the ankles.

"Objection—speculation and baiting," I said, raising an eyebrow, making sure our eyes locked.

"Overruled. Answer the questions. And, there'll be no pleading the fifth, because if you try that sneaky maneuver you'll be treated as a hostile witness."

"What do you want me to say, Mads? That breaking up with you the way I did was a mistake? That breaking up in general was probably the worst decision I've ever made? That I miss you? Still want and need you? That I think about you all the time? How I'm thrilled beyond measure I'm working this case with you and not David? That last night—all of it, not just the sex, felt amazing? How when Jennifer told me she was ring shopping with Doctor No Nuts I felt crushed? Like someone reached into my chest, ripped out my heart with their bare hands, and stabbed it repeatedly. Or, that when we were fighting in my office yesterday all I could think about was tearing off your clothes? Less than twenty-four hours ago, you wanted to pull my arms out of their sockets and beat me to death with them, but somehow we ended up doing a complete one hundred-eighty-degree turn, ending up in bed, making love all night. I love you, Madison. I never stopped and I never will. Everything I declared yesterday was and remains fact," I answered with a sigh.

"So last night wasn't just about sex?"

"No. God, no. It never is with you, but you have to tell me, what do you want me to do? I'm at your mercy, Mads."

"I'm just after the truth."

"I just spoke it, *Vita Mia*," I said, shaking my head. "I don't know what you're doing with Noel, but I'm not a gigolo. I don't sleep with another man's woman. I'm a lot of things, both good and bad, but being the other guy isn't one of them."

"I never said you were and I apologize if I made you feel like one. As for the light and darkness inside of you, you're an amazing person, babe," she said, placing her hand over mine. "My actions over the past twenty-four hours have been selfish. You're the last individual I'd ever want to hurt. I'm so sorry."

Her brilliant green eyes sparkled brightly. Perhaps the touch of her soft, fragrant skin pressed against mine, or the familiar setting, or simply her presence in general caused every emotion inside of me to collide.

"Screw it," I hissed, standing, pulling Madison off of her chair, crushing our bodies together, and taking what was mine. "I need you, *Vita Mia*...so much, and *not* just for this," I whispered in between kisses.

"Can I tell you a secret?" She murmured. Her body twisted into mine.

"Always." The word came out breathy, but yet intense. My fingertips skillfully flicked the buttons on her shirt open.

"I never stopped being yours. Only yours. Always yours. I think about you all the time, and not just when I'm alone."

An involuntary moan escaped my mouth. Madison's admission of still craving me exclusively and her yearning for us to be together burned like the heat of a thousand suns. With a powerful sweep, I picked her up. Her legs locked around my waist. Everything ever required to exist lived inside of this woman. Yes, the situation encompassed a strong potential to become painful, and quickly, but who cared? Growing stronger in Madison's capable hands was all that mattered.

Chapter 6

Madison

Attempting to regain composure after this morning's events proved difficult. It's not that I didn't want to focus on work, my brain simply couldn't. Every time an effort was made to think about something else, Luca's lips, hands, body, words, and sounds overtook my once solid footing. If you'd have asked me yesterday at this time if what transpired was possible, I'd have laughed in your face. But here we were. Part of me wanted to hate him for everything. He broke me to the point of admitting my locked-away inner emotions which caused me to despise not only him, but the traitor within me. However, a much larger part of me wanted to love him. He apologized, acknowledging his mistakes. What more could one expect? You screw up, own it, and do what you can to make things better, which was exactly what he'd done. On the ride to the lab, he reached for my hand and held it. We chatted about his family, what they were up to, and bland topics in general. Nothing we spoke of was heavy and certainly not serious. To my great relief he didn't mention Noel. I wasn't ready to address that issue with him yet or anyone. On paper, Noel was perfect. In my heart, marrying him would be an epic error. A lifetime of constantly feeling something was missing—Luca. If marriage for Noel and me was truly in the cards, sleeping with Luca never would've happened. Instead, I'd have been bouncing off of the walls, rushing out to get a manicure, and waiting for Noel to pop the question. Luca placed his palm on the small of my back as a means to escort me into the building. I had to shake all of the unrest in my brain out so I could concentrate on the task before me—Nick Winters and DNA collection.

Head in the game, Langmore. Playtime is over. You've got work to do.

"Doctor Winters?" I asked a man who sat alone reading a magazine in the stark white, rather sterile waiting room of Metrix Data.

"Yes." He looked up.

His sharp, well-dressed appearance, along with his massive, muscular body, cropped salt-and-pepper hair, bronze skin, one hell of a killer mega-watt smile, and the most stunning green eyes in existence, caused me to take pause. Print pictures and video images did this man no justice. Jillian Winters was one lucky bitch. If he were mine I'd spend most days climbing him like a spider monkey.

"Hi. I'm Madison Langmore. I work for Looking Glass Consultants, a private investigating firm. This is Luca Santino. He works for Newman and Associates." Extending my hand, his warm, thick, strong fingers accepted the gesture. My knees went weak as my legs promptly turned to unstable rubber upon contact.

"Please call me Nick." The tone of his voice was hypnotic.

"We're here to make sure your DNA sample is collected and processed," Luca interjected, placing his frame between mine and Nick's, a classic sign of jealousy.

"Have you found anything out?" Nick inquired.

"I'm working on it. I'm following several strong leads. Your DNA will help connect a few dots, hopefully providing the answers we're seeking. I do have a few questions, if that's all right?" I requested.

"Of course, Ms. Langmore. However I can be of assistance, day or night, let me know. Do you wish to speak here, or would you rather elsewhere?"

"If you're Nick, then I'm Maddy. Are you free after this?"

"For you and this? Of course, Maddy." Him speaking my nickname caused my heart to flutter.

"Why don't you go see if they're ready for us, *Maddy*?" Luca said. He wore a rather unimpressed expression.

Before I could respond, my phone rang. I quickly looked to see who was calling. It was Noel. "Damn it," I hissed.

"Everything okay?" Luca questioned.

"I have to take this. I'm sorry. Be right back." I exited the office. "Hey. What's going on?"

"Good morning, my angel. How was your night?" Noel spoke.

"Okay. Yourself?" I said, attempting to sound as normal and as cool as possible.

"Ehhh. You weren't there. I missed you. How are David and Tara? I assumed you'd be up at the hospital, which is why I didn't bother to reach out. I wanted to give Aunt Maddy some alone time with the newest member of the Langmore family."

"That's sweet. David, Tara, and baby Kate are all doing well."

"Are you free for dinner tonight?" A high level of

hopefulness resided in his statement.

"I can't. I'm actually at Metrix Data with a client. I've got this mess of an assignment that needs immediate attention. I'm sorry." A twang of regret pierced my heart. Noel was a great guy and I treated him without regard or respect last night. Sleeping with Luca shouldn't have been an option until I'd squared things away with Noel. Shoving my emotions back, because I had no time or desire to dive into that right now, I forced a smile.

"Maybe this weekend? I'd like to discuss something with you—nothing bad. Don't worry," he said.

"Yeah. Sure. Let's see how much I can accomplish by then," I said, brushing him off, knowing damn good and well what the something was, and not wanting to deal with it because after what went down last night and this morning I had to say no, and that would hurt him.

"All right. Fair enough. I know how laser-focused you become while working on cases. I wouldn't want to disrupt your rhythm. Who's the job for? Private client?"

"Law firm."

"Really? Which one? I thought David was handling lawyers these days?"

"David is a touch preoccupied at the moment. Until he returns, I'll be doing double duty. This is for Ally Newman."

"One of Jennifer's clients?"

"No."

"Ally's?"

"Technically they're all Ally's clients. However, I'm assisting one of the other attorneys."

"Is it for your ex?" His tone grew harsh.

"Yes, and before you get all cross and bent out of shape, stop. Ally throws us a lot of business. She pays up-front, in cash, never complaining about the cost. I don't get to choose whom I have to collaborate with there. She does. Besides, one day Looking Glass will be mine, so I'd like to keep the existing relationship with her intact."

"You're right. I'm sorry. It's business, not pleasure. Don't work too hard, dear. I'll call you later. Love you." His irritation instantly disappeared.

"I make no promises."

Clicking the end call button, I turned to find Luca standing behind me.

"Oh, Jesus. You scared me," I snapped. My hands clutched my chest.

"Everything okay with Doctor No Nuts?"

"You've got to stop calling him that. Is the technician ready to see Nick?" Luca had been referring to Noel as Doctor No Nuts for as long as I'd been dating Noel. I knew that because Jennifer had told me. Honestly? When she mentioned it to me, a certain sense of satisfaction was had. Obviously, it was a jab from a scorned man at Noel's quiet, nonconfrontational demeanor, but Luca was better than name-calling. Noel was nothing like Luca, which is what initially drew me to him. Neither man was better than the other—just different.

Yeah, but that edginess and masculinity which seeps out of every single one of Luca's pores is what gets you all hot and bothered. There's no way you'd be happy spending the rest of your life with someone like Noel, no matter how safe and comfortable he may be.

Stop. This is neither the appropriate time nor place to be thinking about your personal life. When this case wraps up, clean up your mess. Until then, shut up, brain.

"Doctor Sexy just went back to a treatment room. Want to see if they'll let you in so you can hold his hand? Give you a little more time to swoon?" he drawled sarcastically.

"Jealous much?" I retorted.

Cocking his head and raising an eyebrow, he grinned. With one swift motion, he shoved my back against the wall, crushing our lips together, and kissing me in such a way all logic and reality didn't exist.

"Nah, I'm not jealous *or* worried, *Vita Mia*. I know what you want. How to make your toes curl. How to make you scream. All of the secrets your body holds— I'm aware. Unlocking and releasing your hidden desires—easy. Nick Winters, Noel Wasserman—they're clueless. They can't handle you, but *I* can, and you're aware of that. It's what kept you awake every single night we've been apart. It's what fuels your nightly fantasies. So, with that in mind, this is how our strange little scenario is going to play out. You tell Doctor No Nuts it's over, then you get in your car and drive to my place. Once we're in bed I'll remind you over and over again why you made the right choice," he whispered. His warm breath teased my lips and neck as he pressed his hips against mine. I'd be lying if I said the moment didn't make me want to jump him right then and there.

"Someone thinks rather highly of himself," I scoffed, attempting to play off how accurate his words were.

"Maybe I do. Maybe I don't. Doesn't matter. What does is how well I can read you. I dare you to challenge me, Mads. You know I'm right," he taunted.

"Stop, Luca." I slid out from his hold. There was no way in hell I'd let him know for sure that he still held a substantial amount of power over me. I was already working at a disadvantage with him possessing the knowledge I hadn't fully gotten over him.

"Is that what you want? Me to stop speaking the truth? Me to not say exactly what you're thinking? To not provide all that's craved on every conceivable level?"

"Yes. Please. Thank you."

"Might want to tell your face that, *after* you catch your breath," he said, before abruptly returning to the waiting room.

After a few minutes alone to compose myself, I joined him. We sat in silence for a little over an hour before Nick returned. Once he did, he followed us back to my house.

"I don't want to take up any more of your valuable time, so I'll be quick." I smiled, handing him a bottle of water. "What can you tell me about Noah Lessor that's not in the file Ally provided? I read he was a part of his cousin, Warren Lessor's, cult. He was never charged with any crimes, was treated in a mental health facility, then sent back into society, receiving outpatient services. Because I legally can't hack confidential medical records, and because you're a psychologist *and* someone who lived with him even if for only a short period, can you shed any additional light on Noah? Also, what was his relationship with Sarah Davis like?"

"Do you think Noah is involved?" Nick asked, seemingly shocked by the thought. He shifted in his seat and sat a bit straighter.

"We have reason to believe Noah and Sarah are residing together in a house in Queens. We're unsure of the age of the child in question. All we're certain of is there were diapers in her trash cans and a rear-facing car seat in a vehicle registered to Noah. Best guess is the kid is a toddler, roughly around two years old, but that's solely based on evidence. Is there a possibility he or she might not be yours, but rather Noah's?"

"I suppose anything is possible," Nick said. He appeared to be absorbing this new information. A slight look of disappointment hung from his otherwise flawless face. Recovering quickly, he spoke again. "They didn't interact much. To be frank, Noah didn't chat with anyone besides Warren unless it was absolutely necessary. Even then he offered few words. I thought they were sent to different psychiatric treatment centers. How they hooked up is beyond me."

I scribbled a note to research where each went. "Is there anything aside from Noah being quiet that you'd like to share? The more information you can provide, the faster we can wrap this up, and you can get your life back," I said, hoping he'd give me even the tiniest crumb to work with.

"Anything said would be purely speculation," he warned.

"Of course."

"While being held in Warren's home, I spoke with and attempted to treat the other abductees, but never Noah, or Warren for that matter. If pressed to make an assessment, I'd have to strongly suggest Noah was the victim of childhood abuse. I doubt sexual abuse, but definitely mental, emotional, and physical. He clung to his cousin for everything—guidance, direction, you name it. Noah probably viewed Warren as his savior. I'd also venture a guess that Noah suffered some sort of tragic loss which scarred him. A parent. A lover.

Someone he deemed special or important. Most likely someone who treated him with kindness and affection. I say this because he lacked the ability to connect. Noah wasn't on the spectrum. His cognitive awareness was never called into question. At some point *he* decided to shut off feelings of any kind. Because of that, he encompassed a rather one-dimensional personality. Back then, Warren pulled the strings deciding what Noah could or couldn't do. No thinking or emotion required. Hopefully, the therapy he received taught him how to make decisions for himself—stand on his own two feet without allowing himself to be heavily influenced by those around him.

"As for Sarah, she suffered from Stockholm Syndrome, like the others. She too was abused, but by her ex-husband, *and* she was emotionally disturbed. You have to remember, none of those people were encouraged or taught to deal with and heal from the pain of their pasts. Warren kept them locked away, providing this false sense of security from the outside world. It's been a while since I thought about any of this, but I used to take notes while holding sessions with Warren's prey. There were about a dozen or so leather-bound journals I wrote in. Granted, a lot of the data in them was altered because Warren would read them, but the general nature of who each person was and their basic background is accurate. I'm sure they were taken when the police raided the compound and possibly placed in some kind of evidence archive area. The case has been closed for a long time. I'd hate to provide weak, erroneous information. So much has transpired since then, but if you can retrieve them, I'd be more than happy to go through the material with either of you—fill in the blanks, let you know what's fact and what was changed so Warren wouldn't realize what I was up to," Nick explained.

"I'm on it," Luca said, rising, and walking out of the room.

"Any chance you can recall the names of the other abductees?" I questioned.

"Most of them, sure," he answered, taking a small, black pad and a gold pen out of the breast pocket of his sport coat. Flipping the cover open, he jotted on a blank page. Tearing a sheet from the binding, he passed it over.

I moved closer to him. "I'm not a psychologist, but I did notice a hint of disenchantment when I suggested the baby might be Noah's. If there's something, anything you're not telling me, I wish you would. It will only make this upheaval end sooner," my hushed tone urged.

"Hmmm," Nick said with a smirk. "If you're asking if I have feelings for Sarah, the answer is absolutely no. I never felt anything for her. She was a victim and a patient of sorts. What she experienced on all levels was tragic. Everything that occurred between us was a product of circumstance and survival. If there *is* a child *and* that child *is mine*, then I want him or her. Jill agrees. We'd be able to provide a better, more stable life than Sarah can. Whatever we have to do, however long or nasty the fight, Jill and I won't stop until everything is settled in our favor. The micro expression you witnessed earlier had nothing to do with Sarah engaging in a relationship with Noah. It had everything to do with the complicated, bizarre nature of what's transpired since the moment of my abduction. However, I applaud the catch. Most people lack that talent."

"I can't imagine what you went through and still

have to endure. The question had to be asked. My deepest apologies if my words came across as an accusation, but I wouldn't be doing my job, the job you and Mrs. Winters hired me to do, if all angles weren't explored. Mrs. Winters is a very understanding woman. I have no idea what I'd do if I were ever in her shoes. You're very lucky to have her." I smiled, then tilted my head to the right. Gently, I placed my hand over his.

"She really is, and I am," Nick said, grinning from ear to ear over the thought of his wife. The gesture was touching.

"We'll get to the bottom of this, but right now, go home. Spend some time with your wife and daughter. Let me do the worrying. This isn't my first ride at the difficult investigations rodeo. I'll make sure this gets put to bed in a timely manner," I assured.

"When do you think the DNA results will be in?"

"I'd love to tell you any minute now, but we gave the lab several items to match against you. They can only work so fast. The moment the data comes in, you'll be the first call we make. You have my word."

"Thank you for your time and effort, Maddy. It's truly appreciated not only by me, but by Jill as well."

"That's what we're here for. Should anything come up, or you think of any questions, please, reach out—day or night."

Escorting Nick out, I found Luca in the kitchen.

"The FBI sent all of the evidence to the DA's office about a year after the incident occurred to archive it. I put in a request for copies of Nick's journals. It's going to take some time to find and photocopy everything. It's also going to cost a fortune, which Ally will hate."

"Well, we need them, so she's going to have to cope.

I'm sure she's making a hefty chunk of change off this case anyway. If she can afford to wear two thousand-dollar shoes, I'm sure she's got the money to cover the pop-up expense, *and* I'm certain the Winters' bill will be handsomely padded for this sidebar. Her problem. Not ours. Anyway, while we wait, Nick provided a list of the other abductees' names, and there's a garbage bag full of crap in the foyer screaming for our attention. Glove up and let's get after it."

"You really know how to turn a guy on," Luca said sarcastically as he reached under the sink for two pairs of rubber gloves.

Chapter 7

Luca

I'd spent the past five days and nights at Madison's house combing through evidence, researching the hell out of all parties involved in the house of horrors abduction, only leaving once to grab clothing and toiletries from my place. Countless hours were devoted to this chaotic shit show. Just when we'd think we were onto something, had found a solid lead, it turned out to be an epic waste of time. A rabbit hole of eye-opening, psycho shit.

"Ally's on my ass again, Mads. I've got to send her something." I sighed, removing my reading glasses and rubbing my eyes. I'd done nothing but stare at a laptop screen all day.

"Send her the information we found on Warren. Spin a lie about how we believe it's a viable lead."

"I did that yesterday," I said, exhaling heavily. "And she wasn't impressed. Who gives a shit about him and his tale of woe? The nutjob is dead. He holds no bearing on this current case at all." Warren's mother passing away when he was eleven, his father being an abusive alcoholic, and Warren's short involvement with a Bible-based cult in his late twenties meant squat.

"How about the data on the other abductees? Maybe suggest they *might* have some kind of involvement. Even though we know they don't, it buys us a little more time."

"That's not what she wants."

"Then I've got nothing. Sorry, buddy." She shrugged. Madison was just as frustrated as I.

"There's no connection between Lessor and the Winters? The Locke family? Any of Jillian or Nick's affairs? Friends? Liam Stevens? Charles Downey? Mathew Miller? Their public relations people? Timothy Wilder? The station? Topher Robbins? The police or FBI Agents involved?"

"Nope."

"Damn it. We're missing something. There has to be a tie-in somewhere," I hissed out of massive annoyance.

"Why do they have to connect, Luca? It's completely possible the Lessor-Winters tie-in is Nick's random abduction. Nothing less. Nothing more."

"That abduction wasn't random, Mads. Come on now."

"Whether it was or wasn't isn't our problem, babe. We weren't hired to solve that mystery," she countered.

"Sure, but to figure this current situation out, we need to fully understand the entire story. I don't buy the surface value of this case." Something deep within the pit of my gut urged me that there was far more to the story than what was presented at first glance.

The sound of someone rapping on the front door caused Madison to jolt and me to rise.

"I got it," I said, not wanting her to let someone in the house this late at night. She was mine to protect, and I'd always do so. Approaching the foyer, I peered through the side window. It was Noel. A sizable ball of anger formed in my chest.

"It's for you. Doctor No Nuts," I said, with a hint of arrogance. As Madison and I crossed paths in the short

63

hallway, her head lowered. Yeah, he called several times a day, but she always brushed him off, which pleased me. Now that he was here, I couldn't watch the interaction go down. Debating whether or not to strain an ear to listen in on their conversation ceased when something caught my eye. A roster of names from a local college popped off of the screen. Noah Jacob Lessor, Licensed Nurse Practitioner and Midwife. He'd graduated roughly fifteen years ago, top of his class. Digging a little deeper, I confirmed the Noah Jacob Lessor LPN was the same one in question.

How the hell did you miss that? Maybe if you weren't so hyper-focused on Madison, you wouldn't have shit the sheets. Head in the game, Santino. Good catch, though. This is how the baby was born. He delivered it at home and she never registered the birth with the state. I've almost got you, you son-of-a-bitch.

Quickly firing off an email to Ally sharing the new information, I got up to tell Madison. Unsure if Noel had left, I stopped in the living room. Part of me wanted to bust in on them, drawing attention back to me, but another part wanted to observe their behavior while together. Call it odd. Call it potentially self-inflicting behavior. Call it whatever you want, but assurances were needed that what was happening between us wasn't just for comfort and sex. I held my breath as they spoke in somewhat aggravated tones. Pressing my back to the closest wall out of their line of sight, I eavesdropped.

"So, I guess *Vinny Boombotz* is living here now?" Noel seethed.

"No, he's not," Madison said irritated.

"Well, his junk is all over the place."

"That's because he's a messy slob like most men—

yourself included."

After a series of heavy huffs, he spoke. "Do you want to know what my personal favorite aspect of all of this is? Let me tell you. It's your loser ex walking around in lounge pants *and* no shirt like he owns the joint," Noel hissed. Even though he was insulting me, I gave him credit. I'd never witnessed him freak out before. I wasn't sure he possessed that ability.

"Stop, Noel. We're working a case together," Madison rationalized.

"And that requires him to be half nude in your home? Does that help him comprehend words and phrases better? How would you feel if I neglected to put on my scrubs, then pranced around all day in front of Barbara? I don't like this, Maddy. I don't like *him*. He *needs* to go home. If *you* won't tell him, *I* have no problem doing it. The greaseball leaves tonight. How he passed the New York State Bar Examination is beyond me—scratch that. Dollars to donuts his father probably threatened to pop a cap up someone's ass if he didn't," Noel demanded.

"First of all, your secretary, Barbara, is a seventy-two-year-old grandmother of eight, and your patients are children. If you walked around your office naked, you'd put her into cardiac arrest and would find yourself behind bars. Listen, Noel, I understand where you're coming from, but I have mountains of research to do and I need Luca's help. I'm sorry you're upset, but insulting him isn't the answer. I'm not telling him to leave. You're going to have to find a way to deal with this."

"He's a thug, Madison. His entire family are felons. Why would you ever want to be associated with them? You're better than that."

"Stop it. Enough. First, Luca has never been involved in any criminal activity. Second, I have no idea what you've heard about the Santinos, but they're good people. Frank Santino has lived his entire life without a single brush with the law. Not even a parking ticket is on that man's record. The entire family are stand-up, loyal, loving individuals. Who, might I add, treat me a lot better and with far more respect than your mother. I can't believe you're one of those idiots who believes everything they read and see on television. You've never met them. How dare you pass judgement. Additionally, for the record, I'm not better than them. Neither are you," Madison snapped. Her standing up to Noel and defending me and my family stroked my ego a bit.

"I'm not going to debate the coordinates of Luca Santino's moral compass—forget about attempting to persuade you to listen to reason about *that* family. Obviously, we don't see eye to eye on this matter." He paused, exhaling heavily before placing both of his hands on her shoulders. "When do I get to spend time with you? There's an important matter we must discuss, my angel."

"She's all yours the second we wrap this assignment up," I said, stepping out of the shadows, making sure to flex, showing off my peak physique. "*So, how you doin', Noel?*" I added, using the heaviest, most exaggerated Brooklyn accent one could muster.

"I am *doing* well. Thank you," he said. A sheer and utter look of disdain for having to be in my presence flashed across his face.

"Awesome. Heading to bed, Mads. See you up there," I said, slapping her ass before climbing the stairs. Was it a rude, disrespectful, dick move? Hell yeah, but screw Noel for thinking he was greater than me. I spent my entire life dealing with morons like him. No more.

If you were the epitome of all things great in this world, your girlfriend wouldn't be coming to me—a lowlife, street hoodlum to satisfy her needs and to make her feel happy, alive, safe, and secure. Keep it up and you'll know exactly what it feels like to have a cap popped up your pretentious ass.

Pausing on the top step, an attempt to make out what Noel was saying proved useless. However, I definitely heard him raising his voice. After a few brief moments of him not letting up, I went back down to the foyer.

"Hey, No Nuts, your problem is with me, *not* her. If you've got something to say, why don't you say it to my face instead of complaining like a little bitch to your girlfriend," I said, standing in front of him, hoping he'd throw a punch so I'd be able to pound him into the ground.

"There's no reason for you to be staying here twenty-four seven. You have a home. Go to it. If you and Madison have to work together, do it at one of your offices—professionally," Noel said. A hint of fear danced in his eyes which empowered me more.

Madison hung back, watching the situation play out from a comfortable distance. She was aware of my temper. One false move from this jackass and my fist would end up in his face. Not wanting to risk accidental injury, she created a sizable space—just in case.

"Do I come into your dental practice and tell you how to do your job? Yeah, no. Don't tell me, or Madison, how to do ours. But, if you'd like to make a thing of this right here and now, bring it," I challenged, throwing my arms in the air and advancing dangerously close to where he stood. "Come on. Let's go."

"You think I'm afraid of you?" Noel snapped.

"Yeah, I think you are. How about you show me otherwise?" I hissed, egging him on.

"You're nothing but a disgusting, classless, piece of trash. I don't give a damn who your family is. You're all the same," he yelled.

A split second later, the weak shit came at my stomach with his shoulder, football tackle style. Mid-charge, I shoved him, sending him flying into the front door. Stunned, he attempted to regain composure. Once back on his feet, he tried throwing a few feeble punches, but missed. It became painfully obvious he'd never been in a physical altercation before. Putting him out of his misery, I took hold of his slight frame and slid his back up against the wall. Restraining him with my right forearm across his chest, I spoke. "She doesn't want you. She wants me. Take the hint."

"Enough. What the hell is wrong with you two? Luca, upstairs. Noel, go home. I'm not doing this. Pissing match—over. I'm a grown-ass woman who doesn't need either of you telling me what to do or who to want. Not only are you making fools of yourselves, but you're disrespecting me and my house. If you can't act like adults and control your impulses, get out, and don't come back. I don't have time for this shit. I've got too much work to do," Madison grunted.

"My apologies. When you figure all of this out, call me," Noel answered, adjusting his dress shirt. He turned on his heel and left, immediately.

"Really? You thought throwing down with Noel was a good idea?" Madison questioned the moment the door clicked shut. Her hands found her hips as a look of dark, fierce warning spread across her flawless face.

"I didn't like the way he spoke to you," I said casually, keeping an eye on her body language, attempting to get a read on how she honestly felt.

"It's not your place to protect me."

"That's where you're wrong, Mads. It *is* my place because you are *my* business." My words were dead serious.

"Luca," she moaned in frustration.

"Luca, nothing. Dump him," I urged.

"It's not that easy."

"Yeah, it is. Don't you want us? Or, is this a last fling before the ring? If it is, I'm out," I huffed, attempting to mask my deep-seated fear that we could be over for good this time. I'd just put my biggest concern out there—being used while she mulled over the idea of Noel proposing.

"How dare you? Last fling before the ring? Seriously?" she snapped.

"What am I supposed to think? For days we've been playing house. For Christ's sake, we've been sleeping together every single night. There are only two ways this can go. You break-up with Noel and we get back together, or we stop doing whatever this is."

Madison remained silent, wearing no expression at all.

"All right. I'm going to take off. As for the case, we'll start meeting at my office beginning tomorrow. See you at nine," I said, irritated and disappointed over how this played out. Reaching for my shirt, she stopped the action.

"We both know that isn't what either of us wants, babe," she whispered. Moving closer she placed her hands on my chest. Her long nails dragged over my pecs and abs until her thumbs hooked into the waist of my sweats. "I like you in my house, especially when you're shirtless."

A choice presented—force her to make a decision, or continue proving I was the better man to spend forever with. Had my big brain been thinking properly, opening a dialogue that ended in resolution would've occurred, but the little brain took control. Gently, I pushed Madison's back against the nearest wall. My mouth attacked her swan-like neck while my hands held her arms above her head, forcing this unreal woman to remain in place.

"I want *you*," she murmured.

"You have me, *Vita Mia*." Her body melted into mine with every intimate touch.

"Forever?" Her shoulders and back tensed.

Releasing her, I pulled away. "Is that what this is about? You're afraid I'm going to up and leave?"

Her green eyes instantly filled with tears. "You did it once before. Who's to say it won't happen again? I still want the same things from you. That hasn't changed. I want marriage, a family, and I'd love that from you, but I'm getting too old to roll the dice and gamble on someone who isn't ready for that."

"Mads. No. That's not the case. This time is for life. You have my word. I wasn't ready back then. In hindsight I should've told you that instead of running away, but that doesn't change the fact that I loved you back then and love you even more now. I'd do anything to be with you. I'd do anything for you, always. Walking away from us is the biggest regret of my life. Tell me what you need to feel secure and it's done. Is it marriage?

I'll propose right now. Hell, we can jump on a flight to Vegas tonight and tie the knot." Desperate to establish a face-to-face connection, I leaned down and tilted her chin upwards. She had to see how truthful and serious my words were.

"You saying that is enough—for now," she said, before pressing her lips to mine.

Though not what I wanted to hear, I'd have preferred to have been told, after making mad, passionate love to her, that she planned to call Noel to officially dump him for me, but, for the moment, her statement would have to do.

****

"What should we order tonight? Chinese? Greek? Thai? Diner?" Madison questioned, flopping on the couch the following night. We'd spent hours outside of Davis's house earlier today, waiting and watching, but turned up empty. She and Noah were either securely tucked away inside of the home, or were out doing who knew what. No one approached the property except the mail carrier and sanitation people. What made the situation more frustrating was there was absolutely no record of the child's existence aside from a car seat and a metric ton of dirty diapers—not enough evidence to firmly be sure. Granted, once DNA was extracted and matched against Nick's we'd be aware of far more, but for the moment, our hands were tied. We couldn't even ask neighbors or local vendors about Sarah and Noah. What if one of them mentioned it to them? Lying low while lurking in the shadows was the only viable option—which was maddening.

"How about some Italian?" I said, winking.

"Sicilian?"

"Of course."

"Already had that today—twice," she countered, tilting her head and smiling.

"Well played, but no more take-out, Mads. We're going to be a thousand pounds apiece by the time we finish this case." Trying to keep our conversations as light as possible proved difficult. I wanted answers, but I didn't want to push her any more than I already had. My heart should've been content with the knowledge she pretty much admitted a choice was made—me and us, but until she dumped Doctor No Nuts, satisfaction wouldn't be mine.

"Then what do you suggest?" she asked, throwing a piece of popcorn at my head.

"Very mature. Come on." I got off of the floor and pulled her to her feet.

"Where are we going?" she asked hesitantly.

"Don't worry about it."

She came willingly, but the moment I parked outside of my parents' house, she backed away.

"Uh, no," she said. Her arms folded tightly against her chest.

"Why not? My family misses you. They ask for you often and you've inquired about them several times these past few days. Since we're *almost* back together and you're already familiar with their special brand of insanity, it'll be like riding a bike. Besides, it's a homecooked meal—not something from a carton. Plus, it gets us out of the house for a little while, giving us a well-earned break."

Before she had a chance to answer, my mother came running out to the curb. She always did that when I arrived. I couldn't remember the last time she hadn't.

Sickness, injury—didn't matter.

"Maddy?" she asked shocked.

"Hi, Gina. How are you?" Madison smiled brightly.

"Are you two…?" Her index finger waved back and forth between us finishing the rest of her unspoken question.

"Ma," I started, but she wasn't listening.

"This is wonderful. My prayers have been answered," she said, reaching for the diamond cross which hung from her neck, kissing it, then taking off like a bat straight out of hell into the house, thrilled over what she saw, and surely telling everyone inside while setting another place at the table.

"I'm sorry. You know how she can get. I'll clarify when we go in, or we can leave. Your choice." I sighed. The expression on Madison's face wasn't what I'd hoped for. My family, God love them, could be a bit much to handle, especially the women, but to have an innocent error in judgment be the reason she ran from the prospect of us getting back together couldn't happen, hence the real reason as to why I had provided her with a way out.

Within seconds, the deer caught in headlights look disappeared from her face. Madison sat grinning as her head shook. A slight laugh rolled off of her tongue and out of her mouth. "I forgot how much I love and miss your crazy-ass family."

"So, you're okay with being here?"

"Yes. Of course. It's Wednesday, which means your mom made lasagna. The wine is always strong enough to get you just a little buzzed and the company never disappoints."

Relief washed over me once the realization Madison was all right and comfortable being back around the

Santino clan again sunk in. Walking to the door, she reached for my palm, tangling our fingers together.

"What are we doing here, Mads?" I asked, stopping, closing my eyes, and taking a deep, calming breath.

"Having dinner with your family. Your idea, not mine. Remember?" Her tone was playful.

"No, I know. That's not what I meant." Releasing her hand, I backed away. An abundance of nervous energy caused me to pace in small circles as my thumb vigorously rubbed my beard.

"Then what do you mean?" She glanced up at me through her alluring, long lashes. Her doe-eyed look was the kill shot.

Mustering the balls to finally secure what was mine, I spoke. "I love you, Mads. I'm in love with you. I've always been, and I'm never going to stop. I'd do anything for your happiness, and would gladly exchange my life for yours. I'd sacrifice whatever as long as you were there." I paused, watching for her reaction. Her beautiful, bright irises grew moist. "Don't cry, Mads. Upsetting you is the last thing I'd ever want to do. This is a good thing. I promise."

"Babe," she whispered, pressing her body against mine.

"I'm all in—forever. I probably should be down on one knee—hell, at this point with a diamond the size of Texas in a better location than my parents' front porch, but if I didn't ask you now, I'd regret it until the day I died. This can't wait, because I don't want to wait any longer. Too much time has already passed. Wasting another second would be a sin. Will you marry me, Madison? Will *you* be *my* wife?"

"Are you being serious?" Her frame retreated

slightly, but she remained in my arms. An awestruck look hung from her face.

"I've never been more serious in my life."

A certain radiance I'd never witnessed illuminated from every inch of her being. "I've been waiting for you to ask me that since the first day we met." She beamed.

"Is that a yes?" I inquired. Hopefully, it was.

"Oh my God. Maddy's back. Marie, Tina—Mom wasn't making crap up. She's really here with Luca. Get your skinny ass inside, stranger, and tell us *everything*. Spare *no* detail," my oldest sister, Gia, shrieked with excitement.

Madison pulled away from our embrace, smiled, and shrugged her shoulders as my sisters dragged her into the house, smothering her with affection.

"You're with Maddy again?" my mother asked as I got a drink from the refrigerator.

"I don't know, Ma."

"What's not to know? She's pretty, smart, tolerates, and loves you. You should be thanking God she took you back after you dumped her for no good reason. That girl is your match. I've been saying that since the first time she stepped foot in this house. Your father and I couldn't have prayed for a better partner for you," she said as she chopped peppers into cubes.

"It's complicated."

"You're making it complicated, Luca. Do you love her?" She placed the knife down and turned in my direction.

"Yeah, Ma. I do, but she's dating someone else."

"Then why is she here with you and not out somewhere with him?"

"We're working a case together."

"So? She could've gone off with him and you could've come over here alone tonight." She paused to examine my face. "There's more to the story, Luca. Tell me."

"I don't want to have this conversation, Ma," I said. I put my hand up to stop her from countering.

"We're having it." Giving her classic Gina Santino side-eye look indicating she wasn't going to let this go, no other choice but to spill my guts presented.

"Fine," I huffed. It was easier to give into her will than to fight. The woman wore at least three rings on each hand. If I dared to defy her wishes you could bet your sweet ass she'd crack the back of my head with those brass knuckles. Besides, maybe she had something to offer—an approach I hadn't considered. "Look, you were right. I was wrong. I never should've broken up with her, but it happened, and now it's regretted."

"*But…*" She waved me on.

"I proposed about five minutes ago, okay? Happy? Now you know everything I do."

"What did she say?" She gasped. Her eyes danced with excitement.

"Nothing, because Gia interrupted us."

"You need to talk to her, immediately. Take her in the yard and finish the conversation. I'll keep everyone inside."

"Later, Ma."

"No. Not later. Get your ass outside with that girl and ask her to marry you again. Drop down on both knees and beg if necessary. She's your other half, Luca. If you want her to be yours, not some other man's, go get what you want. Do you have a ring?" she demanded, grabbing the wooden spoon off of the counter and waving it wildly in my face.

"I don't because I wasn't planning on asking her. It just came out. Before you ask, I meant it. I want to marry her, and no, she's not pregnant."

"Of course she's not. Don't be *stupido*. Maddy isn't one of Marco's bimbos. Do you want Nonna's ring to give her? I have it upstairs. She'll love it."

"All I want is for her to say yes."

"Then go talk to her, Luca."

Putting my hands up in the air, I exited the kitchen. When Gina Santino told you to do something, you better do it, or else. Standing at the bottom of the foyer steps, I called up.

"Mads?"

Nothing.

"Mads?" A little louder.

Still nothing.

"Hey. Gia, Tina, Marie, and Madison," I bellowed, clearly hearing the full strength of my Brooklyn accent.

"What, Luca? What do you want?" Tina shouted back.

"Where's Mads?"

"What?"

"Screw this," I mumbled, climbing the flight of stairs. My sisters were all in Marie's old room sitting on the bed, talking in hushed whispers, promptly stopping the moment I entered. Some things never changed. They'd been doing that since birth. The original Italian-American gossip queens of Brooklyn.

"Where's Madison?"

"She went outside to take a call about five, ten minutes ago. Now get out," Tina informed.

My brain paused. I didn't hear the front or back door

open and close, but Madison was always light on her feet, so it wasn't out of the realm of possibility that she slipped past me without me knowing. I checked the back and front yard. She wasn't there. I called her cell, but the line didn't ring. It went straight to voicemail.

"You've reached Madison Langmore from Looking Glass Consultants. If this is an urgent matter, press one for prompt attention. If not, leave a message. I'll get back to you as soon as possible. An email or text is preferred for a faster response."

"Mads, it's me. Where are you? Call me immediately, please."

Going back into the house, I found my parents in the living room. "Have either of you seen Madison? Tina said she went outside to take a call, but she's not there." I'd never been one to panic, but the emotion bubbled to the surface. Her house was miles away from my parents'. Walking from Brooklyn to Long Island would take hours, but what if she called a cab or a rideshare? Maybe being here was too much? Perhaps she overheard my conversation with my mother? Did one of my sisters say something to upset or anger her? Had the impromptu proposal set her over the edge? There were too many variables to consider.

"No. Have you tried her cell?" my father asked.

"Yeah. It goes straight to voicemail."

"Is it possible she went home? Wasn't feeling well? Something came up? Did you piss her off?" he continued, not looking up from his newspaper.

"She would've told me and I would've taken her wherever she wanted to go. Madison knows that. Up and leaving without a word isn't her style."

"You sure?" One eye appeared over the top-left

edge of the periodical.

"Yes, Pop. I'm sure. Madison is aware I'd throw myself in front of a damn bullet for her, so why the hell wouldn't I take her home if she was ill? As for leaving for other reasons, I highly doubt it, but maybe. I don't know." I paced the length of the space, forcing my mind to think of where she might've gone.

My sisters made their way to the living room, stopping, and standing in the doorframe.

"What's with all the yelling?" Marie asked.

"Who phoned Madison?" I said.

"Why?"

"What were you talking about with her upstairs?"

"That's private," Marie clapped back.

My father approached, raising his right hand to stop me from speaking any further, putting an end to the bickering.

"Madison left. Luca's car is still parked outside. Her phone goes to voicemail. We're trying to figure out why and where she might've gone," he said calmly.

"We were talking about Luca. Apparently, he proposed right before they came into the house, which caught Maddy off guard because they'd only just reconnected and he was such an epic jerk in the past about commitment. She said she wanted to tell him yes, but she was worried he'd back out and ghost her again. We all agreed the best move was for her to break-up with Noah, the dentist guy she's been seeing who Luca beat up the other night, before considering Luca's proposal. Maddy is like a sister. We want her to be happy, but we also want to be honest about our opinions. Then, the phone rang. I think it was the dentist boyfriend because she said, 'Hold on, Noah,' and went downstairs. That's all I know," Marie stated.

"Noel. *Noel* is the dentist boyfriend," I said.

"*No*, Luca. She said *Noah*," Tina piped up.

"Are you sure?" Air caught in my throat.

"I'm not a gambler, but I'd bet my life on it," she said. Marie and Gia nodded in agreement.

"What is it?" my mother questioned, placing her palm on my shoulder. Her maternal intuition alerted her to the fact that something was wrong.

"I have to go," I answered rushed, but my father's powerful fist grabbed my forearm.

"Where? What the hell is going on?" His tone was firm and direct.

"He took her. That psycho son-of-a-bitch has her, and if he hurts her, I will end him," I hissed through gritted teeth. I felt my eyes widen as fear settled in.

"Who? Who took Madison? The dentist?"

"Noah Lessor. If she said *Noah* and not *Noel*, then that fucking sick bastard grabbed her, and I have to find her immediately before he does anything to harm her."

"You're jumping to conclusions, Luca."

"No, I'm not."

"Noah is a common name," he reasoned.

"Madison doesn't know anybody named Noah except Noah Lessor—who happens to be one of the people we're currently investigating."

"Perhaps she met someone while the two of you were broken up." He paused thoughtfully. Visible signs the wheels in his head were analyzing random data presented. His thick fingers ran through his salt and pepper hair. His head lowered. "This is related to the case you're working on together?" my father probed, whispering Lessor repeatedly as a means to jog his memory of where he'd heard the designation before.

"Yes."

"Lessor," he said again. "Where do I know that name from?" He'd given up on attempting to remember, and now opened the floor to anyone who could provide an answer.

"The Nick Winters abduction from a while back, but the man who took Nick and all of those people was Warren Lessor, not Noah Lessor. Maybe Noah is a relative? Brother? Son? Does Nick Winters or Warren Lessor have anything to do with the case you're working on?" Gia, my true crime-loving sister, said.

"Winters, as in *Beau Winters*?" my father queried.

"Yeah. That's Nick's grandfather. What does any of this have to do with you, Pop?" I interrogated.

"Marco," he shouted. "Marco. Get your ass out of the kitchen and in here now."

"Oh?" My brother, Marco, materialized holding a plate of food in one hand while the other waved in the air.

"We've got a potential problem," my father said. "Gia, Marie, and Tina, take the kids to the basement. Let them eat and play down there until I say it's okay to come back up. Gina, call Salvatore. Tell him to get over here as soon as possible and to bring some of our friends. Marco, grab your brothers-in-law and find me anyone who saw Madison leaving the property. Look for doorbell or security cameras, knock on doors...you know how to do this. Luca, sit. Rest assured we'll find your girlfriend. Nobody, aside from the boys, under any circumstances, can leave this house. Got it?"

We all nodded in unison. When a riled-up Frank Santino gave an order, you'd be a lunatic not to follow it. Terrified over the possibilities of what may or may not have gone down, the fact my father was on it provided copious amounts of relief. He'd get to the bottom of whatever this was straight away.

"Good." Mumbling a string of obscenities in Italian, he exited the room.

"If anyone can find Madison, it's Pop," Marco assured.

With a curt nod, I turned, suppressing the urge to punch a hole in the nearest wall. Seeing no other option, I too left the space hot on my father's heels.

Chapter 8

Madison

"Oh my God. What are you going to say?" Gia's eyes were wide with tense excitement.

"I want to say yes, *but* it's complicated," I said, still taken aback that Luca had proposed. A year ago, I would've been jumping up and down, but right now hesitation hung heavy. Doubt if he only asked because of the masculine display of territorial nonsense from the previous night bothered me. Was this simply a pissing contest where if he won, he'd go back to his old days and ways, leaving when he realized marriage was the ultimate commitment, a word and concept that freaked him out? Though he suggested that wasn't the case, I couldn't shake the uncertainty.

"How so?" Gia moved closer, taking a seat on the edge of the bed.

"For starters, do we not remember how Luca and I ended? In case you've forgotten, he dumped me, without warning because he apparently 'got scared.' Then, there's Noel."

"Who's that?"

"This guy I've been dating for a while. He's a dentist. Nice enough. My friend, Jennifer, told Luca Noel was going to pop the question. Ever since then your brother has been hot on my ass."

"*Nice enough*? If you're describing him like that,

this dentist doesn't sound like he's the guy who stole your heart. Plus, if he did, you wouldn't be here with Luca, or with Luca at all, and you especially wouldn't be sleeping with him," Tina suggested.

"Who said anything about sex?" I raised an eyebrow.

"Oh, please. You're actually going to sit there and flat out deny knocking boots with him? You do that and let us know how it works out," Tina scoffed.

"Whatever." I sighed, flopping on the window seat. Being in the Santino house felt like home. Luca's family always treated me like family. I hadn't seen these women in well over a year, but here they were acting as if no time had passed at all. The bond we formed never died.

"If Luca screws up again, we'll kill him. Problem solved," Tina added very matter-of-factly.

"Yeah, we will," Marie chimed in.

"Because I haven't seen enough acts of violence lately."

"Has work has been that rough?" Gia asked.

"No. Your brother. He threw down with Noel last night."

"That's hot." Tina smiled.

"Really?" I rolled my eyes.

"Oh, come on. You know it was," Marie added.

"Okay. Fine. Maybe just a little," I admitted, then paused, taking a deep breath. "I love him. I'd consider myself the luckiest bitch alive if we were to ever get married. He's perfect, gorgeous, brilliant, but he's also a weakness. One whose power and hold over me is so strong, he damn near destroyed me when he upped and left. I don't know if my heart can endure another annihilation. I still want things like marriage, kids, the house with the white picket fence, and the golden retriever. I'd like to have that in the near future, which means time is of the essence."

"A little sisterly advice? Because *yes*, you are a Santino sister. Even if you're not with Luca, you'll always be family to us. Break-up with the dentist before you make any major, life-changing decisions. If you need more time to consider marrying my brother, take it. There's no rush. This isn't a race to the altar. You're still pretty young and have plenty of time to have as many babies as you want. Luca will understand if you communicate your thoughts with him. He's always been a fair guy in that respect. *And,* when you finally decide you want to officially become a member of our family, remember, we all look good in rose pink when you're picking out our bridesmaid dresses." Gia winked.

"Who's watching the kids?" I asked, attempting to change the subject.

"Marco's bimbo friend, Tiffanie. We figured since she's about the same age as our children, they'll all be fine. Besides, Mom is down there keeping a lookout. I give her less than a month before he finds a new piece of ass," Tina said, examining her long, French-manicured, acrylic nails, then getting up to peer out of the window. "But we don't care about *Tiffanie* with an *i-e*, not a *y*. We have weightier issues to discuss, like has anyone seen the new neighbor's ass?"

"Since I'm the only unmarried one in the room, I'll be the judge of that. Thank you very much," I said, laughing lightly.

"Not for long," Tina's voice sang.

"*Possibly*, but for now, I'm still unwed," I said, being interrupted by the sound of my cell phone ringing.

The caller ID read Unknown Caller. It wasn't uncommon for work calls to come through as private.

"Hello?" I said, making sure to turn my body away from Luca's sisters, and to retreat to the doorframe.

"Is this Madison Langmore from Looking Glass Consultants?" an unfamiliar voice inquired.

"Yes, this is she. May I ask who's calling?"

Silence.

"Can I help you with something?" I pressed.

More silence.

"If this is an emergency, please hang up and dial nine-one-one. If it's a non-emergency, feel free to call the office. Someone will be there to assist you."

"That won't be necessary. This is Noah. Noah Lessor," he said finally.

"Oh. Hello. Can you hold on for one moment so I can speak with you in private, Noah?"

"Sure."

I gestured with my left hand that I had to take the call while my lips mouthed the word *Sorry*. Leaving the room, I walked down the staircase, and exited the house. Once I was on the porch, I spoke again.

"I apologize for that, Noah. How can I help you?"

"I can't hear you. You're breaking up," he answered, though I heard him crystal clear.

Moving away from the house and toward the street, I asked if the connection had improved. If I wasn't so focused on the call, I might've spotted a gold work van slowing down and stopping in front of me.

"Don't yell. Don't scream. Don't run. Drop the phone and get in," a masculine voice demanded. The man was wearing a black ski mask. He sat stone still behind the steering wheel, looking straight ahead. My body froze.

"Get in." His tone became considerably firmer.

Intense fear overtook every ounce of my mental and physical form. I had no idea what was happening. Adrenaline pumped. My knees shook as my arms tensed.

"You have one second to do what I say before I shoot you," he said, revealing a handgun that was placed on his lap.

Setting the phone on the ground, I did as I was told. Climbing into the passenger seat, I attempted to remember everything my father had taught me about situations like this. Don't attempt to escape, be polite, get to know your captor and surroundings, look for opportunities to help yourself, and remain as calm as possible. When interrogated be cooperative, keep your answers short, don't divulge too much information, keep mental logs of daily activity and movement, no arguing or threat making, and focus on surviving.

"I'm Madison Langmore. May I ask who you are?"

Nothing. He continued driving in silence, making no effort to remove his mask. My brain made copious notations of the path taken. We rode the Belt Parkway to the Southern State, where he merged onto the Seaford Oyster Bay. Eventually he took the exit for the Long Island Expressway heading east. For well over an hour he coasted down the four-ninety-five. Finally, he got off of the expressway. Assuming we were closing in on the final destination, I was wrong. Two rural dirt roads later, we arrived at an abandoned, in the middle of nowhere shack.

"Get out and don't try anything funny," he ordered. His eyes glanced down at the gun resting on his right leg. "Keep your hands where I can see them."

"Okay, but just so you know, I'm not going to run or try to escape," I assured him as I followed his orders.

The moment I exited the van, he dug the barrel of the weapon deep into my lower back. Holding my hands up at my sides, he pushed me to the rickety porch. Leaning around my left shoulder, the unidentified man opened the door. Once inside, after securing a series of padlocks, he told me to sit. A threadbare, brown-and-orange velvet couch was shoved in the corner. My eyes soaked everything in as I took a seat. The area was one open space—rather reminiscent of a summer bungalow. Besides the ancient sofa, a heavy, walnut-stained wooden table with four matching chairs had been placed across the room near a tiny kitchen, which was comprised of a stove, refrigerator, sink, and limited counter space. A twin-sized cot with a dirty, flat mattress, an old television with an antenna on top, a VCR, and various odds and ends made up the remainder of the interior. The entire joint was in dire need of a good, deep clean, and a lot of TLC.

The man moved around nervously, checking his cell phone several times before finding a glass in one of the cabinets.

"Do you want something to drink or eat?" he inquired.

"No. Thank you. Maybe later." I smiled, making sure to keep my hands folded on my lap and clearly visible.

"Do you have to use the bathroom?" He pointed to a pocket door next to the cot.

"No. I'm good."

"I'm not going to hurt you." Though his words were considerably kinder than before, he refused to make eye contact.

"I believe you. If there's anything I can do to help you, let me know."

"Why are you being so nice? Why aren't you trying to get out of here, yelling and screaming? I pointed a weapon at you, which I'm sorry for having to do, but I needed you to listen and come with me."

"Why wouldn't I be nice to you? I wish you'd tell me who you are and what you want, but I'm sure in time you will. You seem like a decent man," I said, trying hard not to show fear while recalling everything I'd learned about abduction situations over the years, but I was truly scared out of my mind. Surely by now, Luca realized I was gone. He probably already called, found my phone, and alerted the police and my parents. They'd find me. For Christ's sake, they were private investigators and Luca's father was a freaking Mafia boss. Between the two forces, any second now they should be busting through the door rescuing me.

"Just call me *darling*, my dear," he whispered, removing his mask.

What the hell?

An involuntary gasp escaped my throat. Not a large person by any stretch of the imagination—standing roughly five feet, seven inches, one hundred forty pounds, and of average body type, the man appeared to be in his late thirties, with sandy-brown, cropped, curly hair, and soft hazel eyes. He wasn't bad looking, just awkward. Now that he'd relaxed a touch, his voice and demeanor mellowed.

"What can I do to make you happy, *Darling*?" I asked cautiously, ready to attack with every ounce of fight inside of me if this lunatic decided to force himself

89

on me.

"I'm confused," he said, taking a seat on the couch, collecting my hands, and intertwining them with his.

"About?" I queried, not pulling away from the gesture.

"I didn't want to do this, but I *had* to. You have to know that I'd never want to scare or harm you—ever, and I apologize again about the gun. Please forgive me, my dear." His eyes glanced down in shame. Darling had some idea of the fine line between right and wrong. A current attack of conscience resided inside of his heart. If the cards I was holding were played properly, this might end shortly, with him allowing me to leave on my own, without injury. However, it was clear to see that he suffered from some sort of mental illness, which caused my anxiety and fears to grow by the second. I couldn't be sure Darling could discern the difference between reality and fantasy, which might cause him to shoot first and feel bad about it later.

"Don't worry about what happened before. It's rearview mirror material. We're beyond it, but, Darling, I have to ask. *Why* did you have to do what you did? Did someone force you to do it? Are you in danger?" Obviously, someone was pulling the strings here and it wasn't him.

"Two reasons. First, she *made* me. You *must* believe me, my dear. I wanted to approach and speak with you, but she said they'd brainwashed you so you wouldn't listen to reason. Second, she said you were, without a doubt, my Rebecca. That *he* lied to my face, and you were really alive, living under a different name. I didn't trust her at first, but after watching you earlier from afar, you look, sound, and act just like her. So you know, I forgive you for being with that man you've been with. It's okay. I understand. She said if I took you here, you'd remember everything and even if you don't, I can keep you safe, unlike last time. I can't lose you again. I'm so sorry for not helping you back then, but I did all I could. I promise I did. Please show me mercy, Rebecca," he begged.

"Okay." I nodded, trying to give off the appearance I comprehended what the hell this lunatic was talking about. *Tread lightly with this whacko.* "Who is *she*? Is *she* trying to harm you? If that's the case, let me help you get away from her. I know people who can provide you with assistance."

"No. You can't. She'll kill you. Tell me you forgive me. I forgave you. It's only fair," he said panicked.

"I forgive you. Let's leave the past in the past." I smiled as warmly as possible under the circumstances.

"Do you mean that?" Darling wanted to believe me, but a healthy amount of skepticism wouldn't afford him that right.

"Of course." Squeezing his hand, I said silent prayers that he accepted my words as truth, even though I still had no clue as to what he did to this Rebecca woman, or even who the hell he was. This man wasn't giving off a murderer vibe, but rather a tragic accident out of his control had occurred causing Rebecca to perish. Had his grief been so strong he couldn't see straight? Was that even possible?

With an ear-to-ear bright grin, Darling yanked my shoulders forward, and pulled me into a tight embrace.

"Don't worry, my dear. Your darling has a plan," he said. He released his hold. A deranged smile clung to his thin lips.

This was bad. Very bad.

Chapter 9

Frank

"What's going on here, Frankie? You've got Marco and my boys running up and down the block, Luca is acting like a caged animal pacing the kitchen, and you have that savage look in your eyes," Salvatore asked, after shutting the door to my basement office. When he and his sons arrived, Gina sent our daughters and their families home. I didn't need their husbands' help. The three men were more of a liability than anything else. Not one working brain cell existed between them.

"Winters." I stood.

"Again with that jackass?" Salvatore said annoyed. "If you don't want to tell him to drop dead, I will. There's no way in hell that I'm going to work another job for him. Out of the question. You're the boss, but, Frankie, come on."

Salvatore D'Angelo had been my right-hand man for decades now. Without him, I'd have been dead a long time ago. For the most part we were on the same page, but ultimately, I made the final call as to what happened and what didn't. Hearing him say I was the boss usually empowered me; however, today it did not. This situation was too close to home for my liking.

"Madison Langmore went missing about an hour ago. I have a gut feeling Winters has something to do with it."

"Luca's ex-girlfriend? Maddy? The P.I.?"

"Yeah. They've been working a case together through Luca's law firm for Nick Winters—the grandson. The one who was sticking his secretary some years ago until the wife found out. Luca and Madison came over earlier for dinner. She went upstairs with the girls. While she was up there, she received a phone call from Noah Lessor, who's connected to Warren Lessor, who was the whack job who abducted Nick Winters. See where I'm going with this?"

"You think Beau is pulling the strings here?"

"I don't know."

"What's the case?"

"All I could get from Luca in between bouts of him losing his shit was he and Madison were investigating a woman named Sarah Davis—one of the women Warren Lessor took. She and Nick slept together while stashed away at Warren's house. Nick believes he's being blackmailed by Sarah, who claims Nick is the father of her child. He's been paying whoever the blackmailer is off until he got tired of it and hired Luca's firm to figure it all out. That's where Madison came in. She found out Sarah has been shacking up with Warren's cousin, Noah, and uncovered evidence of a child living with them. Granted, Beau's only involvement, *that we know of*, is he contacted us a little while ago asking for help, spewing something about the grandson, a baby, and blackmail, but we didn't give him the chance to share much more. My gut strongly suggests he's aware in one way, shape, or form of what's happening now."

"Got it. What do you want to do?"

"Find Madison as soon as possible. If Beau is connected and is aware Madison is back with Luca—

which he probably is, we've got a tremendous problem on our hands, Sally. Lord only knows what he'll do to her to strike back at us through my son." I walked the length of the space unsure of what my next move should be. This wasn't business. This was personal, and personal issues were handled differently.

"All right. Level heads and all that shit," Salvatore said, reaching into his breast pocket, extracting a cigar, and lighting it.

"Luca, my pride, my *figlio preferito*, the one I've done everything to keep away from this life, is now smack in the middle of it. And his girlfriend—she's a good girl. Madison doesn't deserve to be dragged down because of us. For Christ's sake, Luca had just proposed to her outside of this house a little over an hour ago," I snapped out of pure frustration.

"*Basta*. I'm going to have Tony, Jimmy, and Marco pay Beau a little visit. Have them shake him down a bit. Once we know what the old *bastardo* knows, we'll assess from there. I'll have some of our soldiers pound the pavement around here. See if they can unearth anything. It's the only plan we have, Frankie, and we have to start somewhere," Salvatore rationalized.

Nodding, Salvatore called Tony giving him specific instructions. Several additional brief messages later, Salvatore turned to face me.

"Done. Marco found Maddy's phone on the curb. He gave it to Luca to hack into. Other than that, they've got nothing else," Salvatore informed. "What does Luca know about our involvement with Beau?"

"He doesn't, but surely he picked up on something based off of my reaction. He's an intuitive kid."

"We've got to talk to him, Frankie. Fill him in. I

JP Barry

know, I know, you don't want him involved, but it's too late. He's knee-deep in this shit storm with us. Besides, there's no way he's going to sit this one out. If someone took my Donatella, you could bet your ass I'd be on the front lines looking to murder someone—no questions asked."

He was right. The time had come after decades of sheltering Luca to make him a part of something I never sought to. Time might rob me of many things, but the memory of holding my youngest child moments after his birth will never fade. There was something different about him—even my father said so. As he grew into a boy, then a man, that special spark developed into a white-hot fire. Luca was always a happy, easy-going child. As a young man, he excelled at school in a way none of his siblings ever had, and he was handsome beyond words. His only problems were a fierce temper when he was provoked and issues with settling down. Gina and I hoped he'd find balance with Madison, but then he broke things off. With them currently back together, my son's life could become complete. I wanted that for him more than air to breathe.

As a parent, you always want better for your children than what you had. My childhood wasn't bad by any stretch of the imagination. The oldest son of immigrants from Sciacca, Sicily, I knew at a young age what my father did. It wasn't a secret. Luca Santino Senior, my father, was the head of the Santino Crime Family. He formed the group upon arriving in New York and quickly rose to power. As a teenager I ran small, odd jobs for the family. The length, amount, and size of what was expected of me increased over the years, until late May, about twenty years ago.

96

Maurizio D'Angelo (Salvatore's father) and mine were shot outside of the D'Angelo home by a rival family. My old man pulled through—there never was a doubt he wouldn't—but he couldn't carry on as boss anymore. Sadly, Salvatore's father passed away before the ambulance arrived. That's how Salvatore and I got here. We'd been prepped and primed our entire existence for this moment and when it came, I don't know. It never felt right. Sure, there were perks. Our families never suffered a need or want, but at what cost?

I never worried much over my girls. Gina handled the lion's share of raising them. Each ended up becoming a real estate agent, got married, pregnant, then transitioned into becoming stay-at-home mothers. None of them selected what I'd consider worthwhile husbands, but who was I to tell them differently? They were decent men who loved their families, just dumb as hell. So, I hired them as soldiers to make sure my daughters and grandchildren were taken care of. Then there was Marco—my oldest.

Marco had been a hothead from the day his soul came to be. He arrived on his terms—early and screaming. A careful eye always had to keep on him, because one never truly was aware of what lurked inside of his mind. Please, don't misunderstand me. Marco is one of the most giving and generous people alive. He just frequently operated from a position of emotion, not skill or strategy. A real shoot first and don't ask questions later, just bury the body and pretend it never happened kind of guy. I prayed when my time came to pass the torch—something I didn't want to do, but had no other choice but to do, he'd learned enough on how to be an effective, proper leader. For the moment, Marco wasn't even the tiniest bit close to that goal.

"Keep it surface, Sally. Don't tell him too much," I warned.

"You can't shelter him from this world—*our* world, *his* world, whether you like it or not, forever. See how far it's gotten you? It always catches up," Salvatore said.

"What if they kill her? Then what?" The thought of someone, especially someone tied to Beau Winters, causing harm to Madison twisted my heart.

Out of nowhere one Wednesday night Luca showed up to family dinner with this stunning girl. Sure, occasionally he'd bring a woman around, but never unannounced, and never for a meal. The look on that kid's face—I'd never witnessed it before. Pure love and happiness seeped from his every expression. Every action toward her was out of affection and desire. Madison seamlessly blended right into our group. It was as if she'd been with Luca for centuries and had known us forever. She was witty, smart, charming, classy, tough, but above all, her eyes sparkled with passion for my son.

"That's Luca's wife," Gina said the second they left.

I couldn't have agreed more. As the months passed, the bond between them grew tighter and rather intense at times. Two such moments which stuck out were when Madison slipped, breaking her leg while working, and when Luca had the flu. Luca had been over at the house hanging out with Gia when he got the call about Madison. The kid ran out of here like his ass was on fire to get to the hospital. He spent the next six weeks practicing law from her home office so he could tend to the girl's every need, and so she wasn't alone. Before that, in early February, Luca came down with a nasty flu bug. Madison did everything possible to provide him with healing comfort while he recovered. Gina even admitted she herself couldn't have taken better care of him.

However, the one time I mentioned marriage, a sudden fear gripped Luca's words as he stammered out a weak, uneasy answer. He wasn't ready. Then, a few months later, Luca showed up for Wednesday dinner alone. We didn't have to ask where Madison was. We knew. He dumped her. One might suppose the combination of her family not caring much for him, Richard and Donna Langmore thought they were something and my son was Mafia trash, and the pressure from all angles to propose had caught up to him, so, he ran. Did I agree with his actions? Not at all, but it was his life.

The time I spent alone with Madison proved the girl's love and devotion for my son, earning her a place in my heart as one of my own kids, which is why I gave Madison the nickname—all of my children were referred to by terms of endearment, *tesoro*, which means treasure in Italian. She was and still is a treasure. On occasion, I'd swing by her or Luca's house to either fix or drop something off. Most times she was there working. She'd invite me in with a warm smile followed by a tremendous hug. She'd make espresso and we'd talk. Honestly? She was one hell of a private investigator. A few times she even helped me locate someone. Within an hour, she'd have an accurate address and phone number and in one case, a grave location. After the split, I never mentioned Madison to Luca again. Gina was another story. She harped and nagged until Luca exploded into a cacophony of excited utterances, abruptly leaving the house, swearing he'd never return if she didn't stop.

Before Madison's visit today, the last time we spoke was a little after the break-up. She looked like walking death with a pale complexion, puffy eyes, and a red nose. Her hair hung limp as a means to conceal her makeup-less face. I'd been out on Long Island for business and spotted her at a coffee shop. I was unsure if I should approach her or not. Thankfully, she made the decision for both of us.

"Hello, Frank. How have you been?" she said, attempting to hide her inner emotions by grinning brightly.

"*Tesoro*," I said, embracing her and kissing both of her cheeks.

"How are you? How's Gina? Marco? The girls? Your granddaughters?" Madison clung to her fake smile for dear life.

"Everyone is well. How are *you*?"

"Busy with work. My parents are looking to retire soon. They're going to give David and me the business when they do."

"That's wonderful." I said, examining her tragic beauty. "He was wrong. I promise you that one day he will regret his actions and will come crawling back."

"Thanks. I'm going to go now before I start saying things, making myself look like a desperate, heartbroken loser, and worst of all, cry—because I haven't done enough of that already—in front of my ex's father. It was really nice seeing you, Frank. I mean that. Please send all of my love to Gina, Marco, and all of the girls. I'll see you around," she stuttered nervously. Her captivating green eyes, which were filled with moisture, looked everywhere except at me.

"Hey, *Tesoro*, just because you're not with Luca anymore doesn't mean that you're not welcome to come by the house or to speak with Gina and the girls." I paused. "He called you his *vita mia*. Do you know what that means in English?"

"My life," she whispered on the verge of tears.

"Luca is a lot of things, but a liar isn't one of them. If he referred to you as his life, then he meant it. If you're ever in the neighborhood, want to talk, or just crave a good meal, stop by the house. We'd love to have you."

With a brief squeeze of my forearm, she took off into the crowd. To be honest? I was crushed for her.

"Can't think like that, Frankie," Salvatore said, ripping me from my thoughts.

Perhaps he was right, but deep inside I was keenly aware that if anything happened to Madison, not only would it wreck me, it would kill my precious Luca, and that wasn't about to happen.

Chapter 10

Luca

One hour into not knowing where Madison was, all
sanity slipped from my being. My father wouldn't allow
me to do a damn thing. Granted, he had at least three
dozen of his minions pounding the pavement leaving no
stone unturned, but I wasn't out there looking, trying to
piece clues together. My suggestion to reach out to the
Langmores was shot down rapidly by my father. The
only time they were to get involved was if his men
couldn't locate Madison.

Within minutes, Marco found her phone on the curb.
Tossing it to me, he instructed I break into it because it
was locked. Not much suspicious activity was revealed
on the device other than the last unknown call. It wasn't
much to work with, but at least it was something to
explore, keeping my mind active. Had I allowed my
thoughts to travel to dark places, my mother's house
would've suffered the consequence. Desperately, I
wanted to speak with Nick Winters. This was his fault.
If he hadn't fucked some psycho chick...

*Stop. You're reeling. Instead of wasting your time
and energy caged up in this house, do something. Get
your laptop. Research Noah Lessor. See what you can
find or hack—legal or illegal at this point. Call Ally or
Jennifer to see if they can retrieve Nick's journals from
the DA's office. The copies should be done by now. A*

crumb has to be hidden somewhere in his notes.

"I have to get my laptop from the Camaro, Pop. You can watch me go or get it yourself, but I need it," I informed him the moment he came up from the basement with Salvatore.

With a nod, he opened the door, hawking my every move. Once back inside, I went to fast work, first calling Jennifer, who willingly agreed to pick up the copies of Nick's journals and drop them off. I then moved on to investigating Noah, only stopping when Salvatore addressed me.

"Hey, kid. Let's talk. You, me, and your old man," he said.

"Did you find Madison?" I held my breath, fearing they had, and something horrible had happened.

"The boys are still looking for your *fidanzata*. They'll find her."

"That's not good enough. She's out there somewhere with a psychopath and I'm forced to sit here like a little bitch waiting," I yelled. My attitude and tone were totally disrespectful, especially to men like this, but it was how I felt. My raw emotions couldn't be contained. "And, why do you all care so much? Sure, you know Madison, but until I said the name Lessor, nobody gave a damn. You assumed she ran home because she was pissed over something I did."

"Stop," my father warned. "I understand you're upset. She's your girlfriend and you love her. You're worried, but I've got this under control. For the record, regardless of the name Lessor, we still would've been looking for her. Madison is a part of this family. However, that son-of-a-bitch's name along with the shady Winters family involvement is what makes this dangerous. As for you pissing Madison off, well, it was an honest question and assumption."

"Care to elaborate?" I asked, approaching him and raising an eyebrow of accusation. My arms folded tightly across my chest.

"This isn't a courtroom, Luca. You're not allowed to treat me as a hostile witness in my own home. There are things I don't want you to know about. You didn't want this life. You wanted something different, something better. I wanted the same for you. Sometimes shit gets fucked up and tangled, but your old man always knows how to untie the knots."

"Tell me what you did, Pop," I said. There was a heavy sense of warning in my tenor. My fists were clenched to white knuckle status.

"I didn't do anything except provide for my family—which, might I add, includes you." He locked eyes with mine.

"I'm calling the cops and Madison's parents." As I reached into my back pocket for my phone, his forceful hand stopped the action.

"I said no. You have one option, *figlio*—stand down," he barked.

"How would you feel if it were Ma? I love Madison. Sure, I screwed up, but if memory serves correctly, so did you several years ago."

Releasing his hold, he sat. His head lowered and his hands covered his face. I hadn't meant to throw his past infidelity in his face, but the accusation came out. Aside from Gia and me, none of my other siblings knew of the happening. We dropped it because if our mother could forgive and forget, so could we.

"About a decade ago," Salvatore started, "Beau

Winters approached your father. He said his grandson, Nick, was screwing some girl, and the wife found out. He wanted your father and me to make the girl shut up and go away. He feared a scandal would hurt his political career and damage the family name. Keep in mind people like that don't bother with people like us often. They think we're beneath them, only speaking to us when there's a problem. Anyway, we went and talked to the girl. We warned her to keep quiet and handed her a wad of cash and a plane ticket to California. An apartment, car, and job were all lined up for her whenever she arrived at LAX. We go back and tell Beau about the arrangement. It wasn't good enough for him. He wanted us to kill her. We said no because she didn't do anything wrong. Being the other woman isn't a crime. The grandson was the one to blame—acting like a child, hiding behind his grandfather's connections. You play, you pay, right? I don't know whatever happened to the girl—Kelly, or Kathy, or Kimberly, or something like that. Knowing them, they found someone else to whack her. All I know is the bastard stiffed us our payment.

"Fast forward to a few years ago when the grandson went missing. Beau reached out again demanding we find him. We told him no, that he needed a P.I. not us. He begged and pleaded, offering all kinds of money. Who's gonna turn down five million dollars, right? So we sent Marco and my boys to snoop around a bit. They found that weird cult house out east. Marco spotted the grandson on the property, took some pictures, and we called Beau. Do you know that son-of-a-bitch did nothing with the information? Nick's wife, Jackie, or Jennie, or Jillian—I'm shitty with recalling names, almost wound-up dead trying to find his grandson, when all along good ol' Beau knew exactly where he was. He stood at the press conferences like a pussy, fake crying for the cameras. But, that's politicians for you. He was willing to risk his grandson's life to boost his visibility and push his agendas. The piece of shit only paid us half of what he promised us, but your father decided to let it go.

"About a month ago, the old shithead resurfaces. He was saying something about an illegitimate baby his grandson may or may not have fathered. The family was being blackmailed. He wanted us to *take care of* the girl and the baby. We reminded him that we don't handle situations like that, especially when women and children are involved. Beau sniveled on our shoulders again, begging, pleading, and throwing money around, but this time we said no and walked away. Tonight, your father told me that the grandson hired your law firm, who hired Maddy's P.I. company to legally go after the mother and child. Until we find out more information, all fingers point to Beau, and we're dealing with him. Right now, actually. As for Noah Lessor, we'll locate him. I've got some of the guys working on that. He may be on Beau's payroll. He may not. It's yet to be determined. These things take a little time to sort out, but I'm confident we'll know something shortly. Sit tight. Do your computer internet looking-up thing. Let me and the boys do what we do best. Protect our family."

"Hell, no. That corrupt piece of shit isn't going to get away with murder. Give me five minutes alone with the bastard. That's all I want. Five, short, fucking minutes," I raged.

"He *won't*. I've got this under control. Keep your hands blood-free, *mio caro nipote*. You've gotta trust your *zio*," Salvatore said.

"Nah. I think Beau Winters and I need to have a sit-down," I said, dismissing Salvatore's assurance that he had a handle on this. Madison was mine, thus my responsibility. I walked to the front door, but Salvatore and my father blocked it. Inch by inch their barricade forced my feet back into the living room.

"Slow your roll, *figlio*," my father said. "You'll have your revenge in due time, but before that can happen, we've got to be sure over who knows what. Never shoot first. Always ask questions to find out the truth before you slam a cap up someone's ass. Dead men don't speak. Live, scared, tortured ones do. In fact, they can't seem to say enough."

"Excuse me," my mother interrupted. "There's a young woman here to see Luca."

Behind her stood Jennifer holding a large box. Though her normal resting bitch-face expression remained intact, Jennifer's eyes told a different story. She sensed something was amiss. Moving to her, I took the heavy load and placed it on the floor beside the brick fireplace.

"Is everything okay? Is this a bad time?" she whispered, analyzing all parties standing in the room. Truthfully, the scene resembled a still shot straight out of any Mafia movie ever produced.

At that moment I had a choice to make. Lie, and let my family do its job, or second guess them, tell Jennifer everything, and see where the cards fell.

"Family dinner. Jennifer, this is everyone. Everyone, this is a colleague of mine, Jennifer Glick, who also happens to be Madison's best friend."

"It's nice to meet you," my father said with a curt

head nod.

"Likewise," Jennifer responded. "A quick word, Luca, if that's all right with your family? I hate interrupting your plans, but Ally asked me to convey a confidential message," she requested.

"Of course. Take your time. Not an interruption at all," my father said.

As I guided Jennifer out of my parents' house by her elbow, her body tensed.

"Okay. What the hell is going on in there, and where is Maddy?" she demanded.

"Not a damn thing, and not here. Just getting ready to eat." I shrugged.

"Then why did you make me schlep to freaking Brooklyn, and why isn't Maddy with you? She's not answering the phone. Noel hasn't heard from her either. He said the last time they spoke was when he and you threw down at her house last night. Richard, Donna, David, Tara, and Ally all have no idea where she is. I swung by Maddy's place before heading here, and guess what, Luca? She wasn't there, but her Suburban was. Glancing through her living room window, I saw your clothing on her couch and your duffle bag on the floor. *Where is she*?" Jennifer snapped.

"I plead the fifth. Whatever I say, I'm damned. Please, for my sanity and yours, go home."

"Is she hurt? Missing? Tell me, Luca. Tell me, now." A fear so intense visibly surged through her core and straight out of her mouth.

"Nothing is going on."

"You're hiding something. I'm calling the police." She reached inside of her oversized purse for her phone.

"Don't. Give me some time to get a handle on this,"

I urged.

Nervous energy caused Jennifer's legs to shift uncomfortably. "I don't know what kind of gangster shit you and your family are pulling here, but if anything happened to Maddy, even if she has a simple surface scratch on her cheek, I'll make it rain black rain on all of you. As a lawyer who cares about keeping her license, you have one day. If you or Madison don't reach out to me within the next twenty-four hours, I'm telling Ally and contacting the cops. Got it, *paisan*?"

"Since you seem to know so much about my family and their dealings, you should be smart enough to leave, and not look back. I love her too, Jennifer. You're not the only one," I hissed.

"Yeah, I don't think you do," she countered.

"Really? Why would I have proposed a few hours ago if I didn't? For shits and giggles? Do us both a favor, Jennifer, go away."

"What did she say?" A knotted expression twisted her face.

"She didn't answer. So, before you alert the police and start a thing, or have my parents' home swatted in an attempt to ruin their lives, let it go for a few days. Give Madison some time alone to process what's going on," I said, conveniently leaving out several key facts to get her off of the scent.

"Why wouldn't she tell me? Maddy shares everything with me." Jennifer appeared caught somewhere between anger, shock, and disappointment.

"Why would she admit to *you*, someone who can't stomach *me*, someone who's rooting for Doctor No Nuts, that she's been sleeping with, is still in love with, and contemplating marrying her ex, the one who broke her heart? You would've tried to talk Madison out of it, and you know something? Maybe she doesn't want to be."

I'd been treated like a gangster's son my entire life. It never bothered me until that moment. Like a switch flipping on inside of my brain, after decades of repressing and hiding my true self, an evil, cruel, nastiness replaced the lie I'd been living for far too long, yet I was aware deep down this day was destined to be.

"You have until the end of the week, Luca," Jennifer snapped.

"I have as long as I say I have, *Jenny*, and I wouldn't challenge that if I were you. That's a threat *and* a promise," I hissed, before marching back into the house and slamming the door behind me. Sure, she'd come snooping around in a couple of days, but until then, there was work to be done. Jennifer Glick wasn't about to get in the way of that.

Chapter 11

Madison

Four days passed. The ninety-six hours were spent riding a rollercoaster of Darling's wild emotions. Questions as to why he'd done this were easy to answer. Darling was an emotionally unstable, mentally ill man who'd been manipulated into believing I was someone I obviously wasn't, but why this person did that remained a mystery. Was it a distraction tactic? Was this linked to a case I'd worked on in the past? Did this have to do with my current case? If he'd only tell me his real name, I'd have a better idea of what I was dealing with. His face held no clues. Yes, he looked familiar to a degree, but no matter how hard I tried, my brain couldn't place him.

Darling continued to refuse to refer to me as Madison, only Rebecca. The few times I corrected him, he'd either snap and tell me to fight the brainwashing, or he'd sit beside me, stroking my hair, assuring me that in time all of my lost memories would return. In between all of that, he never left the property. Sometimes he'd go outside to take a call, though I could never hear who he was speaking with, nor did I dare ask. He clung to the device like his life depended on it, the keys to the van too, never leaving them out or around. They remained securely in his pocket. I simply assumed he was speaking with *she*. Occasionally, Darling mumbled complaints under his breath about this *she* person, but he never

111

openly discussed her. Inquiring about the identity of the mystery woman was too risky. Who knew if it would set him off? Most times he'd sit at the kitchen table and skim books, occasionally attempting to strike up a conversation about random nothingness with me. As for myself, I went from the cot to the couch, to the table, and back. Darling offered reading materials, a pen and paper, and random puzzle magazines and suggested we could play a board game, but most times I'd sit, waiting for Luca, my parents, or the police to bust through the door, freeing me from this prison. Initially, plotting how to physically attack Darling, as well as various ways to escape were thought of, but I was unsure of exactly how psychotic he was. Plus there was the tiny detail of him possessing a loaded weapon. Doing nothing was the safest option.

Every morning I'd hear a car pull up, a loud bang at the door, and tires crunching against the dirt driveway. The first time this event was experienced, excitement coursed through my veins. Foolishly, I believed I'd been saved. Sadly, it was shortly realized he was working with someone, probably *she*, who was dropping off food and supplies. Most times I only spoke when spoken to, and I did so as politely as possible, but starting another day trapped in this hell hole with hope dwindling that I'd ever get out of this mess wore on my soul.

"My dear," Darling spoke.

"Yes, Darling?" I said, knowing damn good and well that if he wasn't referred to in this fashion he'd experience a rapid mood swing. He'd become sullen and despondent for hours on end.

"I have a surprise."

"Oh?"

You decided to take your nut pills this morning and are going to let me go home?

"You've been wearing the same clothing for a few days. I thought you might like a change." Handing me a heavy, brown, paper bag he smiled brightly.

Carefully opening it, I extracted several items—a knee-length, elastic waist, navy-blue, cotton skirt, a white, short-sleeve T-shirt, an inexpensive ivory bra and matching underwear, tan canvas sneakers, cotton ankle socks, and a small selection of cheap feminine toiletries.

"Thank you. This is a really generous and thoughtful gift," I said, looking him straight in the eyes. His face would haunt my nightmares for life.

"I hope everything fits. Go shower and try it on, Rebecca. Oh, and please leave your hair down. You know how much I love when you do that," he encouraged.

With a nod, I went to the tiny bathroom. At first, I worried he'd try to sexually assault me, but it appeared he respected and cared about whoever this Rebecca woman was too much to cause her any sort of physical harm or pain. If my soul needed to find a silver lining, that would've been it. A heavy sigh escaped my lungs as I slid the flimsy bar lock shut. The space barely had enough room for me to turn around in. It reminded me of a restroom you'd find in an RV—a small standup shower with a microscopic toilet and vanity. To sum it up, a claustrophobic's worst nightmare. Darling stood outside of the door, poised and waiting for me to rejoin him.

"Oh, Rebecca. You're an absolute vision."

"Thank you." I produced a faint smile before I began my walk back to the couch until lunch, when I'd join him at the table.

He gently took hold of my wrist. "I thought maybe, if you're not too tired, we could clean up a bit together. This place isn't good enough for you. I apologize for that. Once she says it's safe to leave, I'll find us something spectacular—I swear. For now, making this environment as homey and comfortable as possible will help to bridge the gap." In his own warped, childlike way, he loved this Rebecca person with every fiber of his being. The hope, passion, and sheer joy in his expressions spoke volumes.

"I don't doubt that, Darling. Tidying up sounds like a good idea." A part of me felt bad for this poor, sick man. He truly meant no maltreatment. *She* was influencing his thoughts, perhaps with threats or employing fear. Whatever the case, a stranglehold over him existed by her hands and her hands alone.

"Wonderful. There's another surprise for later. I'm going to make your favorite dinner, *and* I was able to get a copy of your favorite movie."

He wanted assurances that I was happy, that he'd done the right thing. Still tremendously skeptical of what the mental breaking point for Darling was, playing along had to occur.

"How kind. I can't wait. Thank you."

"All right, my dear Rebecca. Let's get to work," he spoke, clapping his hands, then rubbing them together rapidly.

An eerie chill formed at the base of my spine, chasing a combination of fear and defeat all the way up to the tiny hairs on the back of my neck. Surviving this physically wasn't what irked me most. Getting through this without losing my sanity is what taunted my every thought.

Chapter 12

Luca

"If we report this to the police, we'll have to tell them she was here. They'll think one of us had something to do with it. Our family isn't exactly in tight with law enforcement. Next thing you know, one of those pigs will be at the front door with a search warrant, dragging all of our asses down to the station to question us for things we aren't even a part of. Furthermore, once they're in the house—who knows what the ratbags will find? These jackasses have been looking for a reason to get in this home legally to take us down. This is it. We're screwed," Marco ranted, pacing the length of the basement. His arms waved wildly in the air.

"Madison was kidnapped and all you can worry about is the police and how this will affect you?" I yelled.

"Oh, no, no, baby brother. How this will affect *all* of us—you're included in that mess. Could you please talk some sense into him, Pop? Luca has no clue how the other half lives. School him, quickly, before we all end up behind bars."

"Boys, stop. No one is going to jail, Marco. We will find your girlfriend, Luca. Take a damn breath while Salvatore and I figure this out," my father said calmly.

"What's to figure out? Jimmy went to Maddy's house. She's not there and there's nothing inside to clue us into anything. Not a soul has entered the home either

115

since she vanished. Trust me. The guys gave the property a good once-over. They swept for fingerprints and footprints too. I told Jimmy to shelter in place, see if anything pops up. Carmine is sitting outside of Maddy's parents' house. Zero movement. Rocco is watching Looking Glass. It appears the Langmores are conducting business remotely. Joey and Sammy have eyes on her friends, as well as the dentist's condo and office. Again, not a damn thing. Her phone is a dud, except for that last blocked call, which Colombo over here can't crack the case of. With no hardcore evidence to prove it was Noah Lessor, her cell is a dead end. Since no one around the neighborhood has any kind of surveillance cameras, who the hell knows exactly what happened? Traffic cams show a mess of cars, any of which she could be in. We have one eyewitness, Mrs. Monticello from across the street, who says she saw someone who may or may not have been Maddy get into a gold, silver, or possibly white van, but she wasn't sure because she's what? A thousand years old, blind as a bat, deaf as a post, and was snooping through her blackout curtains.

"I sent Dominic and Tony over to the address Luca gave us for Sarah Davis and Noah Lessor. No one was around. They said the front door was open, so they took a peek inside. Furniture was there, but clothing and personal items were all gone. Dominic spoke to one of the neighbors who told him a young man and woman with a small child had been living there. She saw them when she got home from work several days ago, but she hasn't seen them since. Apparently, they kept to themselves. She couldn't even tell him their names.

"We shook down Beau pretty damn hard. He's clueless. Believe me, Pop. If that bastard knew something, we would've squeezed it out of him. I don't think this has anything to do with our past involvement with Winters. It's a coincidence Luca was assigned to work on the Nick Winters baby mama drama case. Madison's disappearance isn't tied to Beau or us. That's not saying Davis or Lessor aren't guilty, it's saying Winters is not—*this time*," Marco said, throwing his hands up in defeat.

"If we don't find her right now, Jennifer Glick from Newman and Associates is going to report it to the police," I said, no longer able to ignore the texts and calls from Jennifer. It had been four days since Madison went missing. The last message I received was a clear threat that Jennifer intended to follow through with.

If you don't produce Maddy tonight, I'm making the call, Luca. Her parents are riding my ass, and I can't keep dodging bullets to protect you. Enough is enough already. I understand the situation, but she wouldn't stay away for this long. That was what she wrote.

"There's no such thing as a coincidence, Marco. *Especially* not in a situation like this. If Beau is clean, there's something or someone else attached to him that caused this. Go speak with the grandson, Salvatore. See if you can get anything out of him. As for Ms. Glick, distract her until Salvatore returns," my father instructed.

With a curt nod, Salvatore took off out of the back-basement door.

"How the hell am I supposed to do that, Pop?" I hissed.

"Meet her at your office. Talk to her. Use that charm of yours while feeding her a line of bullshit. Marco will text you the second Salvatore returns. We'll go from there."

Disagreeing with this tactic, but doing as told, I called Jennifer. It was after hours, but she'd still be burning the midnight oil. Cautiously, she agreed to speak but warned if the conversation didn't end with a phone call to the authorities, she'd do it herself. Forty-five minutes later, we sat across from one another at her desk. I'd prepared myself for the worst, but shockingly enough, she was quite mellow, dare I say rational.

"I'm aware of your family's *business*, Luca. I haven't said a word to Ally, Ryan, or anyone about Maddy, but it's been four days. Maddy would've reached out to one of us by now, even if she was still processing her dilemma. We both know the chances of finding someone alive after two days are slim to none. Maddy's parents called three times yesterday and twice today. I ignored the first few messages, but answered the last one. They wanted to know if I'd seen her. I couldn't lie, so I told them what you shared with me—that the two of you were back together and you proposed. Your proposal spooked her and she disappeared. I'm sure they're still in the process of reaching out to people and searching for her, but real soon they'll start looking for you, then file a missing person report. As an attorney, as *your* attorney, because only a moron would think he didn't need one right now, I advise you to call the cops and tell them the absolute truth. Jump out in front of the Langmores with your version of what went down. I'm sorry to be the bearer of obvious news, but, Luca, you're going to be suspect number one. All eyes will be locked on you, no one else. With that in mind, before we contact the authorities, is there anything I need to be made aware of?"

Shit got real, fast. My head spun. Police? Lawyers?

What the hell?

Who in their right mind would believe I'd do anything to cause harm to Madison?

The cops and everyone else who loves Madison, that's who. Your family is a little too well known for all of the wrong reasons. You and Madison have been broken up for some time. Suddenly, you're working a case side by side, spending days on end together. She's with Noel, a reputable pillar of society, who was about to propose. Without a doubt, he'll share that bit of information with the police. He'll also make them aware of the physical altercation that went down between you and him at Madison's house. You've been sleeping with her—unprotected, might I add, which means your DNA is inside of her and under her nails. Noel and the Langmores will scream rape. Plus, neighbors could corroborate your presence at her home. A prosecutor is going to spin this against your favor. They'll suggest you wanted Madison. She said no. You forced yourself on her. Took it too far, hurt her, then ran to Daddy to clean up the mess. You haven't been in the office for over a week. Aside from a few calls to Ally, no one's seen either of you, except your family. Madison spoke with her parents, brother, and Noel while we were together, but opposing counsel will say those calls were made under duress. Furthermore, you're confident this is true because it's exactly how you'd play it. Jennifer is right. You need to tell the truth and lawyer up, immediately.

"I love Madison, Jennifer, and I swear I didn't hurt her."

"I know you do and didn't. However, I can't help her or you unless I'm made fully aware of what's going on. Give me the smallest bill you have in your wallet."

"Here," I said, extracting a fifty from my billfold and sliding it across the desktop.

"With this exchange of money you're accepting and retaining my, Jennifer Lynn Glick of Newman and Associates LLP, legal services. I'll draft a contract when we're through here, but as of this moment you're covered under lawyer-client privilege."

"Okay." After a heavy exhale, I began. "Since Madison and I started working the Winters case we've been sleeping together—like I told you outside of my parents' house a few days ago. The sex was consensual, but unprotected. At times it may have gotten a little rough, meaning my DNA is one hundred percent inside of her and possibly under her nails. She also may have some minor bruising and there might be minor tearing or inflammation on her female parts. I've been at Madison's place around the clock, only leaving once to pick up clothing from my home. Her bodily fluids are probably present on my sheets as well. Us *living together* was a mutual arrangement. When we discussed me leaving, she didn't want that and proceeded to come on to me so I'd stay, which I did. The evening before she disappeared, Noel swung by. We got into it with fists and words. I don't know what Madison's plans with Noel are, but I did propose before she disappeared. She didn't respond because when my sisters realized she was at the house, they swarmed her. They were all close when we were dating. I didn't take Madison to my parents' home to hurt her or bury a body, but rather because I thought if I could recapture the old us, show her how we used to be, do the things we used to do, she'd realize how much she missed it, and maybe she'd remember how much she loved and wanted me, not Noel. Popping the question wasn't premeditated. It just came out of my mouth, but every word I spoke I meant. It's selfish, I'm aware. I also know that getting involved with and sleeping with another man's woman behind his back is screwed up, but again, Jennifer, I'm in love with her.

"Madison went upstairs with my sisters while I spoke with my mother in the kitchen. My mother encouraged me to finish the conversation with Madison and get an answer to my proposal. When I went to find Madison one of my sisters said she stepped outside to speak with Noah on the phone. Not *No-el*, but rather *No-ah*. As in Noah Lessor from our current case, unless she knows of another Noah that's not listed in her phone or email contacts. I'm cognizant of this because after I realized she vanished, my brother found her cell lying on the curb. Overriding the password wasn't difficult. Aside from an ancient neighbor whose credibility would be called into question due to the fact her vision, hearing, and memory are compromised, no one saw anything. Not a soul was on the street, nobody has doorbell or security devices, and traffic cams show a mess of cars, any of which Madison could've been in."

"None of that points any fingers at you, Luca. So, unless there's more to the story, I have no idea why you've been sitting on your ass for days. As an officer of the court you're aware of this. So I have to ask, what's the holdup here?"

"Noah Lessor is attached to the Winters family. The Winters, more specifically Beau Winters, have questionable ties to mine."

"Illegal?"

"Depends on how one looks at it."

"Unpack the bag."

For thirty minutes, I explained how all of the pieces to the crazy puzzle fit together. She sat in silence, soaking in every word.

"Okay. I see how this could get complicated and why you're worried. Did anyone in your family have any knowledge you were working for the Winters?"

"Initially, no. After Madison disappeared and the name Noah Lessor came out they made the connection."

"Were you aware of your family's interactions with Beau Winters?"

"No. Again, not until Madison disappeared. That's when my uncle told me." I paused. "My last name may be Santino, and my family may have a poor reputation in some circles, but for the record, I've never been involved in any of their business dealings, I know nothing about what they do, they don't tell me a thing, and they're *not* bad people. They've been going nuts looking for Madison these past ninety-six hours trying to bring her home quickly and quietly."

"Paying off a girl, offering her money, a car, an apartment, a job, and so on to keep her mouth shut we can dispute as hearsay. Nick Winters engaging in an affair is illegal. Adultery is still a crime in New York State—Class B misdemeanor, but that's his problem, not ours. As long as your family didn't cause any harm to the woman, I can work with that. Beau's request that they commit criminal activity and your father declining the offer also doesn't put anyone in your world in the wrong. Again, it's hearsay. The authorities should only be interested in the matter at hand—locating Maddy. They might care about what the Santinos have done in the past, possibly build a side case, and they'll more than likely want to search your parents' home, so if they've got any skeletons lying around I'd get rid of them. If the cops don't find anything, your mother, father, sisters, and brother will not be deemed suspects."

"The cops will plant evidence. You know that as well as I do. Come on, now. We're handing them the Santino Crime Family, a Mafia group they've been after for decades, on a silver platter," I countered.

"They won't if Ally and I are in the house when they're there, which we will be. They'll never be left in a room alone. I'll have your parents' house packed with attorneys from this firm. Your sisters' homes too. You have my solemn word. We protect our own in this office, Luca. You'd do the same for any one of us. I'm to assume you're place is clean, aside from the sheets?"

"Yeah." She wasn't wrong. With attorneys hawking the cops every move they wouldn't be able to do a damn thing other than their rightful jobs—no extracurricular nonsense. The time had come to bite the bullet and make the call. I looked down at my hands. Too many conflicting thoughts and emotions smashed into one another inside of my once sharp but now exhausted brain. This situation had grown out of control. Something had to be done to bring Madison home, but at what cost? I ran the risk of not only losing her, but my family as well.

"I can't imagine what's rattling around in that beautiful mind of yours at this very moment, but what other options do you have? Too much time has passed. Maddy's parents, brother, and boyfriend are actively searching for her. Either *you* go to the authorities, or *they* will. Let the first person to report this be you, *not* them. Reach out to your parents first, then we'll call the police together. We're going to tell them you waited before filing a report because you thought she left your parents' house and was avoiding you because you proposed and that might've freaked her out because she was dating someone else, but after a few days when she wasn't answering your calls, you came to me to see if I was aware of Maddy's whereabouts. At that point, you decided a report had to be made because I told you she hadn't spoken with her parents either, whom I'd been in communication with. Also, tell them about the argument with Noel.

"As for the Noah Lessor involvement, that conversation you had with your family about the Winters never happened. You know nothing. All you're going to share is your sister said Maddy took a call from someone named Noah, and that exact name is the name of someone attached to a case you're working on with Maddy, which no one except the two of you and a few of us here at this office have any knowledge of. She went outside and never came back, but you didn't become aware of the communication with Noah until later on. Hand her cell phone over to the police. Explain it was found on the curb by your brother. That he thought it was a random lost device, and tried to gain access to it in order to find the owner. When he couldn't, he tossed it somewhere, forgetting about it. You happened to stumble across it and recognized it as Maddy's. This will explain his fingerprints. Yours are easily justifiable. The rest is the cops' job to figure out."

"What have I been doing for the past few days?" I questioned.

"Working from home because you couldn't get your head in the game to come to the office, and recently trying to locate Maddy."

"My father isn't going to go for this," I said, running my hands aggressively against my face. Jennifer's cover story, though partially true, appeared flawless to the naked eye.

"Do you want me to speak with him?"

"No. He won't trust you. I have to do it. Give me a few minutes. Okay?"

"Hold on a second. Did you find anything in Nick's journals?"

"Nothing we didn't already know. He never treated Noah. He only observed his behaviors. A few notations pertaining to Winters's speculation Noah had been a victim of abuse were included. Apparently, he was quiet, easily startled, a follower, non-violent, and a loner. He hung on every word his cousin spoke. As for Sarah Davis, he diagnosed her with Stockholm Syndrome, personality disorder, and an emotional imbalance. She was a victim of domestic violence. Winters suggested she had the potential for violent tendencies based off of her mental instability, which was showcased in Jillian Winters's live feed when Davis went after Nick with a cleaver in the kitchen. However, in her defense, when pushed or threatened enough we all have the ability to snap and turn into something we're not. It's human nature."

She nodded, swallowing hard. "Make the call."

Once I was alone inside of my office, my feet rooted behind my desk. My hands used the surface for support. The thought of Madison and how we made love for the first time on that very spot caused my right fist to slam into the wood. Had I known back then that she'd be abducted because of me and my family's involvement, I never would've touched her. Never. Several deep breaths later, my tense fingers dialed my father.

"Listen, Pop. Madison's family and friends are looking for her. They're going to alert the authorities. Either we do it first, or they will. I spoke with and retained a lawyer here at the firm, Jennifer Glick, the woman that was at the house the other day. She instructed me on how this needs to play out in order to keep you, Marco, and the rest of our family out of it. We don't have a choice anymore, unless in the past hour someone found her or figured out where she is." For a hot second my emotions clung to false hope a new development occurred in my absence.

"What's the plan, Luca? What did this lawyer tell you?"

After explaining everything, he begrudgingly agreed, suggesting he'd speak to his people to coach them on what to say and do. Hanging up, I placed a second call to the precinct by my parents' home.

"Desk Sergeant Flanagan speaking."

"I need to report a missing person. She may have been abducted," I said. My voice trembled. I was petrified in a way I'd never experienced. My stomach churned in anticipation of the police finding something and my entire family going down for a crime they didn't commit. All I could think was, *was this worth it? Was being with Madison again worth the shit storm you and your family are about to endure?* Sadly, at that moment I didn't have the answer. I think that may have bothered me the most.

Chapter 13

Luca

I sat alone in a dimly lit interrogation room for well over an hour wondering who was watching my every move behind the double-sided glass. Appearing calm waned and waxed. At times my foot tapped against the dirty, bird-shit-green colored, linoleum floor. The dented, cold, steel chair wreaked havoc on my lower back. Other moments were spent pacing while I yanked at my hair and beard, mumbling to myself. I'd circle the metal table several times, stopping to glance out of the barred, wired glass window. The sun descended, leaving the alley view pitch black. Jennifer waited in the lobby for my call, texting me every few minutes.

"Sorry for keeping you waiting, Mr. Santino. It's been a busy night. I'm Officer Anton," the uniformed man spoke, as he entered the room. A light blue folder and cup of coffee were placed on the table. His demeanor appeared rushed, like he had better things to be doing than his actual job. "Please, sit."

Doing as told, I sat across from him.

"You're here to report a missing person," he added, flipping through his papers, eventually looking up from the file. "Walk me through it."

In one long breath I explained the events leading up to Madison's disappearance, conveying exactly what Jennifer coached me on.

"Could it be she's just not answering *your* calls? Perhaps she doesn't want to be bothered with you, or anyone? Maybe she needs some alone time?"

"I have no way of contacting her. As previously stated, Madison's cell is at my parents' house. My brother found it on the curb. He had no idea whom it belonged to until I saw it, recognizing it as Madison's. She's not home, with family, friends, or at work, but her SUV is parked in the driveway of her house. I've knocked on the door many times, as has her friend Jennifer, who's been in contact with Madison's inner circle. No one's seen or heard from her in nearly five days."

"But *you* haven't touched base with her family, friends, or boyfriend?"

"I already told you, the only person I've communicated with was her friend, Jennifer Glick, who is sitting in your waiting room and is a colleague of mine. I'm sure by now Jennifer has told Richard and Donna Langmore, as well as other members of their family, and Noel Wasserman—Madison's boyfriend about what's been going on. I don't have a close relationship with any of them."

"During the year you dated Miss Langmore, you never developed a rapport with her family?"

"Exactly how does one develop a rapport with people who don't care for you?" I challenged.

"So, you and Miss Langmore dated, broke up, and are now intimate again?"

"Yes. I asked her to marry me right before she disappeared."

"Were these intimate encounters consensual?"

"Are you insinuating rape?" My voice darkened

tremendously.

"I'm not insinuating anything, Mr. Santino. I'm trying to create a data story, which means covering all angles."

"Of course they were consensual," I scoffed, making a face of disgust. "What kind of man would I be if I forced myself on a woman, especially one that I love?"

"How did Miss Langmore appear the last time you saw her?"

"Totally fine."

"She wasn't upset, stressed out, or nervous over anything?"

"To the best of my knowledge, no. If she was, she never said anything."

"The night before she disappeared, you and Noel Wasserman engaged in a physical altercation in her home?

"Yes, we did. I was at Madison's house and he didn't like it. When Madison refused to tell me to leave, he became upset. Noel got loud with Madison, which was what caused us to have words. *He* threw the first punch, *not* me. Madison broke it up, and he left. I stayed. She wasn't angry afterward. We spoke about getting back together, to which she appeared to be okay with the idea."

"So without speaking to any of her close connections, it's your belief Noah Lessor has something to do with this?" Anton asked, scanning the last page in the folder.

"Possibly. My sister clearly heard Madison say Noah *not* Noel when she answered her cell phone at my parents' home. The only Noah I'm aware she knows is Noah Lessor, who is part of the assignment we're currently investigating through Newman and Associates, my employer, with the assistance of Looking Glass Consultants, Madison's family business."

"All right. I'll dispatch a few of my guys to Noah Lessor's last known address and see what we can find. In the meantime, do me a favor and write down a list of your whereabouts for this past week and any person who can corroborate," Anton said, sliding a cheap, blue, ballpoint pen and a piece of yellow-lined paper across the table.

"Hold up," I said as he made his way to the door.

Anton turned. "Yeah?"

"I want Jennifer Glick, my attorney, sent in."

"We're not charging you with anything, Mr. Santino. There's no need for a lawyer. You're simply filing a missing person report."

"If that were truly the case, why ask me for the names of people I've spoken with, or places I've been to since Madison disappeared? Why ask questions, then rephrase them, or conveniently leave out key details, or alter already known facts? You're prepping to put a target on my back and are trying to get me to trip up while retelling the story. It's all part of building a case. I've seen this move enough times in my personal and professional life to know. You're going to keep me caged up here for hours because that's how you think you're going to break me, get me to admit I had something to do with this—which *I did not*. While I'm sitting it out, you'll have one of your friends watching me through that glass right over there, monitoring my behavior which truly reveals absolutely nothing. All it tells is a person's threshold of patience during a stressful time while alone, but you people have a way to spin that. Make the narrative suit your needs to stamp the file closed. If I pace or rage out of frustration, I'm guilty. If I sit quietly, I'm guilty and labeled a sociopath by some halfwit quack of a shrink this department employs who obtained their degree from a local online community college. Either way, you've already pointed a finger at me.

"As all of this is going down, you're going to send some of your men to Sarah Davis and Noah Lessor's house, but you're going to find nothing because they already moved out. How do I know this? I'm working a case that involves them. When your cronies return with the news, that'll be another strike against me. Then, you'll dispatch more officers to my family's house. You know who I am and who they are. This is the department's way into their home, legally. They've done and know nothing, but that won't matter because while you're there, you'll find or plant something to open an additional investigation, forgetting about this one, conveniently placing the blame on them and me. Two birds, one stone, and a nice, shiny commendation for you from the boys upstairs. You'll make this your fame case, and all the while Madison Langmore is out there, somewhere, possibly hurt or dead, but you'll bury that so deep in paperwork no one will ever remember or will ever call you to task over fake evidence, which will somehow magically disappear from lockup. The file will go cold and you and no one in this place will care, but I do and I always will. So, when I ask to speak with my attorney, it is my right to do so, because I know how this place operates. In case you forgot, I'm a lawyer. A lawyer who's well-versed in criminal and constitutional law," I informed.

"I'll have someone bring her in," he answered. His

eyes scanned me up and down before he closed the door, leaving me to my own hell.

Thankfully, within minutes, Jennifer was escorted in. Calmly, she placed her briefcase and purse on the table.

"I've spoken with your family. They're good. I've also reached out to Richard, Donna, David, and Noel. They'll be here shortly to provide statements. Officer Anton and I chatted briefly, and I reiterated Noah Lessor needs to be investigated beyond a simple search of his home. Ally is aware and is also on her way. We'll be acting as co-counsel for you. She will hand over all of the paperwork the office has on the Winters case. Let the police do what they need to. Don't give them any fuel for the fire. I'm worried too, but level heads prevail. No one in this building has anything to charge you or your family with. However, should something come up, Ally and I will represent them immediately. Obviously, you're a suspect, as is your family, and anyone else Maddy is tied to, but that's the way this goes. Once enough evidence is provided and alibis are confirmed, you're off the list. Now, we wait. It's going to be all right, Luca. I've got your back and can assure you beyond a shadow of a doubt, no one will be screwing with you today, or any day for that matter, as long as I'm your attorney."

****

Sliding the key into my front door, I'd never been as happy and relieved to be home. Twenty-four long hours in a police station, trapped in the same room with only supervised bathroom breaks, coffee and water, no food, had worn on my entire being. My body craved a shower, a meal, and sleep. Upon exiting the station I was instructed to not leave the state. Like I'd do that now?

Leave New York with Madison missing. Yeah, sure—okay.

As I walked out of the building I saw Madison's parents, brother, and Noel huddled on a bench in the lobby. Donna's eyes were red and puffy, imbibed with fear. When they glanced in my direction, anyone, even the blind, could clearly see they blamed me. No words were spoken as my feet just kept walking beside Jennifer. When my car pulled out of the lot, through the rearview mirror I saw her go back inside.

Giving into basic needs, I cleaned up, ate something, and hit the sheets, waking late morning the following day. There were several unread messages, emails, and missed calls on my cell phone, but none were from Madison or the police. Only work crap from clients and check-ins from family. Heeding Jennifer's warning to not act suspicious or go rogue but rather to fake normal and do my usual routine, I showered and went to the office. Sadly, even there, everyone stared the second my body got too close to theirs. After I shut my office door, the tears I'd been holding back poured out. This had become too much. The blame and guilt inside of me consumed me. I'd put the one person I loved more than anything at risk because I'd been an epic asshole in the past. None of this would've happened if I'd just left Madison alone, worked the case, and allowed her to be with Noel without interfering.

"Mr. Santino?" someone asked, knocking. I couldn't decipher the owner of the voice.

"Come in," I answered, wiping the moisture from my cheeks with the back of my right hand.

A stunning woman in her early forties, impeccably dressed, with long, auburn, beachy-waved hair, the bluest eyes I'd ever seen, and pushing a stroller entered.

"Can I help you?"

"Hope so. I'm Jillian Winters. I believe you're the attorney who's been handling my and my husband's lawsuit? Luca Santino?" She paused to examine my body language. "Are you all right?" Her captivating sapphires scrutinized my face.

"Of course. It's nice to meet you. How can I be of assistance?" I said, ignoring her concern and gesturing for her to take a seat.

"Ally told Nick and me about what's going on with the private investigator working the case. I'm sorry to hear this," she said, parking the stroller beside my filing cabinet and sitting.

I nodded, sifting through papers, extracting the Winters files. "It won't affect anything. For personal reasons I'll be recusing myself from this, but whomever Ally assigns to pick up where Ms. Langmore and I left off will be just as on top of it as we were."

"I'm not concerned about that, Mr. Santino. What I'm worried about is the missing woman. What did you and she dig up?"

"Ally would be the best person to have this discussion with, Mrs. Winters," I said, not willing to share the intimate details of what I knew. Our families were too intertwined, and not in a good way.

"If I wanted to speak with Ally about this, I'd be in her office with the door closed, not yours, but yet here we are." She raised an eyebrow. "I'm well aware you're Frank Santino's son. I knew who you were before agreeing to allow you to handle my case, and I didn't care. I still don't because you're the best at what you do. Double undergraduate degrees from Harvard in psychology and criminology, summa cum laude, graduated top of your class from Yale Law School, editor of the *Yale Law Journal*, writing several published pieces for them yourself, all culminating with you obtaining a perfect score on the bar exam. I researched you. You're no idiot. Those details matter, *not* your DNA. However, when a man named Salvatore comes to my home requesting a meeting with my husband, and when I find out my grandfather-in-law, father-in-law, and brother-in-law were shaken down by a gentleman named Marco Santino along with several of his associates, connecting the dots wasn't too terribly difficult. What's going on here, Mr. Santino? How do all of these pieces fit together? More importantly, what's Nick's involvement?"

"Listen, Mrs. Winters, I know you want answers and for this mess to wrap up so you and your husband can move along with your lives, but it's a process which takes a little time. Please rest assured, the work Ms. Langmore and I conducted was comprehensive and thorough. Whomever Ally selects to finish this off will seamlessly be able to transition into the case without pause. By day's end a new team will be in place. As for Salvatore and Marco, I have no idea what you're talking about," I guaranteed, praying this response would appease her and she'd leave me the hell alone.

I've got no time for your crap, lady. I don't care about your shit either. The love of my life is missing, possibly dead because your husband had to stick his dick in some lunatic, which, might I add, wouldn't have happened if his scumbag grandfather told you, or anyone for that matter, where he was, because he knew. My brother told him right before Beau screwed my father over.

The sudden thought of *my* Madison deceased caused a surge of emotion. Jillian Winters had to get out of my office and now, or else she ran the strong chance of becoming acquainted with nasty Luca Santino, and that's a side no one wanted to see.

"Again, I'm not bothered by the change of venue. I'm not even bothered by the impromptu visit we received from Salvatore—who was extremely polite and professional, or the Marco Santino beatdown on Beau, Tag, and Jackson, none of which has been reported to the police, nor will it. All I'm after is figuring out how our families are tied together." This woman wasn't taking the hint it was time to go. She sunk deeper into the chair, crossing her legs, and settling in for the long haul.

"I don't feel comfortable discussing this further," I said, closing the folder.

Leaning in she whispered, "If anyone understands what you're going through, it's me. Been there. Done that. Could write a book about it. By the way you're acting I'm going to guess Ms. Langmore is someone special. Perhaps a girlfriend or lover. If you have questions about anyone involved in my case, ask, because I'd bet my life I have the answers."

"All right. Tell me about Noah Lessor. I read through your husband's journals from when he was abducted. Not much is mentioned about Noah. Doctor Winters didn't frequently comment on him either." Tilting my seat back, I waited for her reply, desperately hoping she'd fill in some of the elusive blanks.

"All I know is he was Warren Lessor's cousin. He acted as a right-hand man of sorts for Warren. He and Warren slept upstairs while the rest were in the basement. Noah didn't interact much with the others. When I found Nick and everything went down, he stood there doing absolutely nothing. However, he did go willingly with the paramedics. If you haven't seen the video of it, I encourage you to give it a watch and see it for yourself. If you already have, I suggest giving it a more detailed inspection. I can have Charles Downey send over a clear copy if you'd like. The only other thing I can think of was Nick said he didn't view Noah as a threat or a danger. He felt with the right treatment plan and medication, Noah would heal. That he was capable of being okay again."

"What about Sarah Davis?"

"She's a nut cake." The sentence slid right out of her mouth without thought. A true gut reaction. Though she might suggest her husband knocking boots with some other woman didn't bother her because it was an act of survival, deep down it did, and bad.

"Care to elaborate?"

"You realize Nick and I hired Ally because of her, because of what she's doing to us, right?" Jillian did nothing to conceal her demeanor and body language. All signs pointed to a clear portrayal of an angry woman.

"I'm aware."

"Do you think she or Noah had anything to do with Ms. Langmore's disappearance?"

"No comment."

"Off the record, counselor." One well-manicured eyebrow rose.

"I don't know," I lied. "What can you tell me about your husband's grandfather, Beau Winters?"

"No comment," she countered.

"There's nothing you'd like to offer up?"

With a sigh, she spoke. "Beau and his wife are the only two Winters who never treated me poorly to my face. As a journalist and member of their family, I've studied his career and can say with one hundred percent certainty the country loves him."

"What about you? Do you share the same sentiment?" I pressed.

"He's just as shady as the others. He just hides it better than most. I can't say for sure because I have no concrete proof, but I truly believe he knew additional information he chose not to share about Nick's disappearance. Call it whatever you'd like—a gut feeling, woman's intuition, but after all of the dust settled down he made a few odd remarks. Nick picked up on it too. After Salvatore's little visit, we're confident there's more to the story, and the Santino Family plays a role in some parts of it. However, we decided it's best to let sleeping dogs *lie*." Reaching for a slip of paper and pen from my desk, she carefully wrote something down before sliding the note back.

"Look here. If Ms. Langmore isn't there, try the other address. If Sarah or Noah have her, chances are they took her to one of those places. They'd view them as safe houses. Both are out of the way, far off the beaten path. Liam Stevens and I had to do some serious digging to find them ourselves. I don't believe Beau had anything to do with this. I could be wrong, but I highly doubt it. He may have gotten the ball rolling years ago with your family, but this situation feels different. I hope this helps. If you have any other questions, or require anything at all, give me a shout. Good luck, Mr. Santino," she said, throwing her purse over her shoulder and backing the stroller out of my office.

Looking at the document, a few choices presented. Take off now and do my own investigation. Tell my father and family, dragging them down further. Reach out to the Langmores or Doctor No Nuts. Call the police. Or tell Jennifer and see what she advised.

I clicked the spacebar on my keyboard, and my computer sprung to life. Several clicks and a cross-reference confirmation later, I reached for the phone, and dialed a number my fingers knew by heart.

"Hey. It's me. I've got two addresses where Madison may be. I'm heading to you now."

Chapter 14

Madison

"Wasn't that a fun memory, Rebecca?" Darling asked.

"Yes," I said, unsure of what the hell he was talking about. We cleaned the shack non-stop for two days, only breaking to sleep, eat, and shower. All the while he rambled on and on about things he and Rebecca had done, hoping it would jog a memory. News flash—I'm. Not. Her. In order not to upset him, I simply nodded or agreed. It did, however, seem as if he and she shared many light-hearted adventures. I couldn't figure out if Rebecca was his wife or girlfriend. Obviously, they didn't have children, because he never mentioned any. He also hadn't tried to kiss or touch me once other than a hug or a fleeting brush of the hand. He respected her. He was in love with her. Had he not been totally out of his freaking mind, I would've thought the dynamic between the two was sweet and old fashioned.

"I saved something for you, my dear." He moved closer, handing me a picture.

The paper was frayed at the edges, suggesting it was an older print. A seemingly young Darling stood beside a woman I swore was my doppelganger. The resemblance was uncanny. This had to be Rebecca, and now I fully understood why this mentally unstable man thought I was her.

"Do you remember that day?" he asked. His voice filled with hope.

"It was at a carnival?" I said, drawing on clues from the photo. Rebecca held a gigantic, stuffed panda bear, while a Ferris wheel appeared behind them. Both beamed with joy and happiness. Their expressions exuded great love and deep intimacy.

"Yes," he delighted. "See? Your memories are returning."

I forced a smile.

"I have more photographs. Would you like to go through them?" Though he posed the suggestion as a question, it wasn't. He wanted to force recollections down my throat. Quite frankly, I couldn't stand another minute of it.

"Could we not focus on the past right now, Darling? Could we maybe do something else? It's starting to wear on me a bit," I requested as sweetly as possible.

"Of course. I'm sorry. I should've realized you'd need a break. Between all of the cleaning and memory jogging you must be exhausted. I pushed you too much. Please, my dear, sit. Would you like to watch a movie? Eat something? Take a nap? Read? Whatever you'd like, let me know."

Before I could answer, the sound of bags being dropped on the porch caused my body to take a step back. It was *she* doing the morning delivery. Attempting to peek out of the window was useless. The woman always wore dark sunglasses, a hooded sweatshirt, and a bandana wrapped around her nose and mouth. She worked swiftly, throwing the packages, and jumping back into the car, taking off like a bat straight out of Hell. I never caught a glimpse of her vehicle. I only heard the tires crunching against the dirt. She probably parked out of range so even Darling couldn't view it. Opening the door a crack, he dragged several totes into the shack. He quickly shut the door and locked it.

"Let me put those away," I offered hoping maybe she left a receipt or some sort of hint in the bag, clueing me in to who she was or exactly where I might be. All I was sure of was we were somewhere out on the east end of Long Island.

"No, no. Sit. Rest. Relax."

A sense of defeat settled inside of my heart. Little bursts of hope were experienced during the days spent here, but as quickly as they came was just as fast they'd vanish. Today, the will to keep going didn't exist. I felt broken. Done. Hopeless.

"I think I'm going to take a nap, Darling," I said, lying on the couch, turning away from him, and covering myself with a blanket.

"Do you feel all right, Rebecca?" He sounded concerned. "If not, let me check you out."

"I'm fine. Just tired."

"Okay, but if for some reason you decide later on you're not well, I can write you a prescription and have it picked up."

"You can write a prescription?" I questioned.

"Of course I can. Don't you remember? That's how we met—at school."

"Yes, you're right. You can. My brain is exhausted. Forgive me," I said, settling into the couch, closing my eyes, and praying this would end soon.

"I didn't want to say anything, Darling, because I didn't want to upset you or cause you any worry, but I have an awful migraine. About a year ago my doctor prescribed Ubrelvy. It really helped stop the pain almost instantly. Could you possibly call that in and get it here soon? Please?"

An idea struck me. If Darling wrote a prescription with my real name it would definitely alert my parents, Luca, or whoever else was looking for me. A little over a year ago I was stuck on what felt like an impossible assignment. I couldn't find the person in question and not for a lack of trying. The slippery bastard kept eluding me no matter what I did. One afternoon Luca's father came over to my house to hang a light fixture. Luca wasn't there, but when he finished, we sat at the table, chatting over a cup of coffee. He asked me what was wrong. I told him. His advice was pure genius. He said to check pharmacies. Big box stores had systems that were linked together. Smaller ones I'd have to cold call, but since everyone got sick at one point or another, it wasn't impossible my target had as well. Furthermore, he said drug stores sold a wide variety of everyday items. Individuals often ran out of toiletries and needed to eat. Since most people paid using a credit card, tracking them from that transaction would be a cakewalk from there. Added bonus? All pharmacies had security cameras. Frank continued to suggest only real, true, career criminals knew how to cover their tracks. Some random person off the street like the idiot I was searching for would slip up, and quickly. A half-hour later, I found my guy purchasing allergy pills, body wash, and a bag of chips with a Visa. If Darling did that, it would at least be a helpful breadcrumb. As for the Ubrelvy, my sister-in-law had taken it for migraines. It was the first invisible illness and drug combination that came to mind.

"Absolutely, my dear. I'm not mad, but going

forward, you must tell me these things. I can help. I never want you to feel bad or suffer," he said. Immense care dripped off of each of his spoken words.

"It costs a lot of money without insurance, which I have, just not under Rebecca, but rather under Madison."

"Don't worry about the cost. You rest. I'll phone it in."

Slumping back down onto the pillow, the defeat which quickly left moments ago returned, with a vengeance. This was it. I was stuck here with Darling for life.

Chapter 15

Luca

"Yeah, Luca, I know where this is. It's all the way the hell out east on Long Island," Marco said, scratching his head. "Where'd you find this anyway?"

Refusing to reveal Jillian Winters as the source, no other choice but to lie presented. If Marco knew the truth, he'd blow up and make a thing of it.

"From files at work. This address was where Warren Lessor was holding all those people. The other one was listed as a place of interest by the FBI when they were investigating the Winters abduction, but it never amounted to anything. It was deemed abandoned, but was owned by Wilbur Lessor, who upon his death left it to his son, Warren. Both properties are now legally Noah's. It's worth looking into. If you don't want to go, I'll handle it myself."

"There's no way in hell that I'm allowing you to do this by yourself." Marco paused thoughtfully. "You tell the police about this?"

"No. I'm telling you and Pop. Right now the cops think I'm to blame. Due to lack of evidence, they haven't been able to charge me or anyone for Madison's disappearance *yet*, but I hacked into their system about an hour ago. Madison's parents, brother, and boyfriend all accused me. Most of their statements were pure lies, but truthfully, I'm not shocked. Richard and Donna think

I'm the scum of the earth and Doctor No Nuts is pissed I've been doing his girlfriend. It's only a matter of time before I'm arrested on some trumped-up, bogus charge."

"I never cared for Dick and the wife. They always looked down on us like we were low-life street thugs," Marco sneered.

"Richard and Donna can kiss my ass. The dentist too. Forget about them. These properties are about a half-hour away from each other. I'm going to call Salvatore, then we're going to get in the car and take a little ride. Have you heard anything about the girl, Sarah Davis? Anyone find her yet?" my father inquired.

"We're asking around," Marco said.

"You do realize there are two unmarked cars outside of the house right now. The second we make a move, especially with Salvatore and the others, they'll be all over us like flies on shit. They snapped at least three dozen pictures of me entering the house," I reminded him.

"This isn't my first lap around the horse track, Luca. We all drive the same make and model car with tinted windows. Our license plates are similar too. We'll gather here and leave at the same time after swapping vehicles with one another. Once we get on the highway, we'll scatter. The cops won't know who's who. By the time they get backup and figure it out, we'll be long gone. We keep our cell phones at home and use cheap burner flip ones which have no location tracker on them. They also have scrambler chips in them so the Feds can't tap into any of our communication. Salvatore disposes of them when we're done," he explained.

"On it, Pop." Marco reached for his phone and exited the basement.

"Aren't you afraid of getting caught?" I asked, completely baffled by his calm demeanor.

"No. Marco will speak in code with Salvatore. I might not be a desk jockey, but I've always made sure your mother, sisters, brother, and you were safe and sound. Circumstances chose my path in life. I don't regret it. As long as I'm at the helm of this family, nothing bad will ever happen, and if by chance it does, there's no situation in this world I can't find a way out of." He paused. "I'm going to find your girlfriend, Luca. Whatever it takes, she will be returned to you. Whoever has her, they'll pay. If they hurt her, I promise they'll regret it. I've always been rather fond of Madison; you're aware of that. I'm mindful of how much she means to you. If you love her, we love her too. Trust, and have faith in your old man. Now, get your ass in gear and get ready to go."

Fifteen minutes later, twenty-four of us got into six cars. Exactly as my father said, once everyone merged onto the highway going west towards Manhattan, we split; three cars went towards New Jersey, and three went back over the bridge. Between traffic and erratic city driving, we shook the cops quickly. Once we were on the Long Island Expressway, we stopped at a local diner.

"Get out and go to the white, Chrysler minivan. Get in the back. I'm going to park this out of sight," my father instructed.

Doing as told, I followed Marco.

"Hello, boys," Salvatore's deep, scratchy voice spoke once we got inside the vehicle. The rather large man smoking a cigar looked odd sitting behind the wheel of a vehicle designed for a soccer mom.

With him were his two sons, Jimmy and Tony. A

second later, my father slipped into the passenger seat. The two men nodded at each other and Salvatore took off. The next hour dragged and was filled with mindless small talk. When spoken to I responded, but I mainly kept my eyes on the road making sure we weren't being followed. Thankfully, we weren't.

"Look alive, *bambini*," Salvatore said, pulling onto the gravel driveway of a rather large, neatly kept, plantation-style house.

The same small, blue, cheap, compact car Madison and I saw outside of Sarah Davis's home in Queens was parked off to the side.

"They're here," I said. My right hand reached for the door handle. I was ready to jump out and I was fully prepared to attack whoever with whatever force was required.

"Slow your roll, Luca," my father cautioned. His dark, warning eyes glanced at me through the visor mirror. "We do this my way. *Capito?*"

Annoyed, I shook my head in agreement.

"Jimmy, Tony, and Marco, go around back and find a way in. Luca, you're with Salvatore and me. I assume everyone's covered except Luca?" my father ordered.

A sea of *yeahs* filled the car.

"Covered?" I questioned.

"Ever shoot a gun, *nipote*?" Salvatore asked.

"Of course he has. He's *my* son," my father scoffed. "Take this. It's loaded. When you turn this knob down, the safety clicks off. All you have to do is point and shoot, just like I taught you. Here's an extra loaded magazine. Keep it somewhere you can access it quickly and easily. We only fire a weapon when it's absolutely necessary and we always wear gloves."

"I know how to shoot a gun and what the rules are, Pop. Can we go now?" I demanded while sliding a pair of thick, black, leather gloves on that Tony had tossed on my lap, then securing the weapon in the back waist of my pants.

"Let's do this, boys. Make your *papà* and *zio* proud," Salvatore instructed.

Quick as lighting, in stealth, Marco, Jimmy, and Tony headed to the rear of the house. I followed behind my father and Salvatore. They approached the front door and knocked. Moments later a young woman with long, blonde hair and large, brown eyes, holding a toddler answered. Beyond a shadow of a doubt I was one hundred percent certain this was Sarah Davis. How could I be so sure? Aside from a few minor cosmetic details like weight, hairstyle, makeup application, and clothing choice, she resembled the person I remembered seeing on the Catholic school website when this shit show began. Add the vehicle parked outside to the mix, and I'd gamble my life on it. The desire to pounce all over her, demanding answers, caused such a surge, remaining in check and standing perfectly still proved a feat.

"Hello, ma'am. I'm Paul Martin from First Choice Realty. These are my associates, John and Luke. We've been visiting some of your neighbors asking if anyone is interested in putting their home up for sale. It's a seller's market, and we have several motivated clients who'd love to get their hands on anything out here. They're willing to pay top dollar, cash deals, quick turnarounds," Salvatore said, reaching into his breast pocket, producing and handing over a business card.

"Not interested, but thanks for stopping by. Have a nice day," she said nervously, giving the card back.

"Is your husband home? Maybe he'd like to hear what we're ready to offer?"

"No, he's not. Sorry," she said, attempting to close the door, but my father's left hand stopped the action.

"Oh, we think you'll be extremely sorry if you don't let us in," he said, making sure his jacket opened just enough for her to see his holstered gun.

Sarah froze. Absolute terror resided inside of her eyes. Her pupils dilated at such a rapid rate, I thought she'd faint on the spot.

"We don't want to hurt you or your child. We just want to talk, Sarah," Salvatore added.

Turning to run, she stopped dead in her tracks when she spotted Marco, Jimmy, and Tony standing behind her.

"What do you want?" she screamed.

Entering and shutting the door, I approached her. "Where's Madison Langmore?" I demanded.

"Who?" Sarah's voice shook with fear.

"What about Noah Lessor?"

"I don't know who you're talking about."

"Really, Sarah? That's the game you want to play?" I taunted, literally backing her into a corner.

"Again, I have no idea who any of these people are. I don't even know who *Sarah* is," she insisted.

"Think harder, because if you don't, I'll find a fun, but painful way for you to remember," I growled, leaving no space between her body and mine. I'd never raised a hand to, nor ever struck a woman, but if this bitch kept pushing me, she'd become the first.

"The driver's license in your purse seems to think you're Sarah Elizabeth Davis, and the picture looks curiously like you as well. Additionally, the deed to this house was transferred to Noah Lessor upon the death of his cousin, Warren Lessor, also known as the whack job who abducted eighteen, possibly more, people, yourself included. Plus, that's Noah's car outside. So, we'll ask you again, in case you suffered a temporary bout of amnesia. It could happen, right? Where's Noah Lessor and where's Madison Langmore?" Marco spoke, wedging his body between mine and hers and taking control over the situation. Reaching for the child, Jimmy pried him out of her arms. In all of my years as Marco's younger brother I'd never witnessed him behave as calculated and powerfully before. Usually, he acted like a hothead with a short fuse and was always eating something. I wasn't sure what to make of him, or how to process what I saw, never mind felt.

Nothing. Silence.

"I'm a real patient man, Ms. Davis. We all are, but time's up. Tell us or find out what happens next. I promise, you won't like it. Neither will your little boy." He paused. "You know, I read an interesting article recently that said children, especially toddlers, who witness acts of violence at a young age grow up to be psychopaths. This poor kid won't stand a chance. He'll have two strikes against him. The first being his mother's whack job genes."

"I don't know where they are. Noah took off after he found out Nick was suing me because Nick thinks my child is his. Nick also believes I've been blackmailing him—which I haven't. My son is Noah's. Neither one of us want to deal with Nick ever again. I ran too. That's why I'm here. Search the house if you want. No one aside from me and my son are here." Her frame trembled.

"Liar. You've been blackmailing the Winters. They

got tired of your bullshit and hired a lawyer, who in turn hired a private investigation firm to look into you—see if you were telling the truth. When you heard from their attorney, you panicked. Then when you saw Madison snooping around your house in Queens, you had Noah stash her somewhere and took off here to hide, ride out the wave, but guess what? As easily as I found you, the police will as well. If you want to make it out of this alive, start talking," I hissed.

She stood stone still. Her face was devoid of all color.

"Times up, lady. Give me the baby, Jimmy," my father said. Once the child was in his arms, he continued. "You've got the other address. You four go. We'll stay here and will keep an eye on this one. Call the second you find anything. If we need to get out quickly, we've got her, her keys, her identification, her kid, and Noah's car. She's not going anywhere."

With a nod, Marco, Jimmy, Tony, and I left. Thankfully, Marco drove the minivan like he stole it, booking it to the second location in record time. The dilapidated shack hidden deep within the woods resembled something straight out of a horror movie. Overgrown trees and shrubbery suggested no one had been there in a long while. My heart sank. There was no way anyone was here. A ticking sound coming from Jimmy caused me to look alive. Using a series of eye and hand gestures he drew everyone's attention to somewhat fresh tire tracks and footprints. Jutting his chin out while pointing two fingers at us, he cued Marco and me to go around back. Lowering his hand, he wanted us to do this quietly.

Cautiously approaching the rear of the structure I

tried to peer inside of one of the windows, but they were so old, dirty, and fogged up, it was impossible. Sneaking around to the other side of the shack, Jimmy pulled us down.

"There's no back door and the windows are painted shut. The only way in or out is through the front," Marco whispered.

"Do you see anyone in there?" Tony asked.

"Nope," Marco said.

"Okay. We get one chance. On three, Tony will kick the door in. We attack SWAT-style—guns out ready to fire, back to back. It's more or less one large room with nowhere to hide. If anyone comes at you, shoot. If anyone spots Maddy, grab her and get the hell out," Jimmy instructed.

As we moved into position, the sound of four safeties clicking caused a chill to shoot up my spine. Sure, I'd handled weapons before, but I never pointed one at a human being. Only tin cans and paper targets. If it came to blows, could I take a life? Did I have it in me, even with Madison's wellbeing hanging in the balance? I never viewed myself as a weak man, but this was different. Throwing a punch and breaking someone's nose was an entirely different animal.

"Get out of your head, little brother. Stop overthinking this," Marco cautioned.

"One, two, three," Tony mouthed.

Once the beast of a man knocked the door down with a single thrust of his foot, everything after happened quickly, a little too quickly to keep up with.

The sound of a woman shrieking and a man screaming for us to get out of his home cut through the silence. To the right, Jimmy had the man pinned to the wall by his throat. To the left, Marco held the woman in a protective stance, using his body as a shield.

"You're okay, Maddy. I got you. You're safe," Marco said loud enough for me to hear him.

Sprinting to where they stood, I pushed my brother aside. Madison's face was white with fright. Her body quaked. She was barely able to hold herself up. Taking her by the waist, I immediately bolted for the door.

"Don't hurt him," Madison's voice begged while we stood in the threshold.

"We just want to get to know your friend, Maddy," Tony spoke. "Is your name Noah Lessor?"

No response.

"He's not well, Tony. Please, just let him go," she plead.

"No one is going to take her from me again. Rebecca is mine," the man hissed as he struggled to breathe.

Reaching into the man's back pocket, Marco extracted a brown, leather wallet. "It's Lessor."

"Why did you do this?" Tony shouted.

Again, silence.

"Answer me," Tony demanded.

After a brief pause, Lessor opened his mouth to speak. " 'Then they will go away to eternal punishment, but the righteous to eternal life.' " Matthew 25:46."

With one swift motion, Lessor grabbed the gun secured on Tony's waistband, positioned it inside of his mouth, and fired.

Chapter 16

Madison

I remained on the couch for most of the afternoon, pretending to be asleep. Darling went in and out of the shack several times, checking on me every so often. Not allowing my brain to take me to any more dark places, I fixated on the true identity of Darling.

"I'm going to shower, my dear. Before I do, is there anything I can bring you?" Darling questioned.

"No, thank you," I answered with a sigh.

"I won't be long," he said, before closing the bathroom pocket door.

My eyes wandered around the space, finally stopping once his unattended wallet was spotted on the dining table. Surely a license or credit card had to be inside. Granted, it wasn't a huge victory—getting my hands on his cell phone or the keys to the van would've been a tremendous win, but this was still a triumph, I hoped. Why he didn't take the billfold into the bathroom was beyond me. Perhaps he simply forgot. Typically he never left any of his personal effects carelessly lying around, but who was I to not take advantage of this opportunity?

The moment I heard the shower water turn on, my feet lightly crept across the floor. An old, beat-up, brown, leather wallet sat perfectly still, waiting to purge its secrets. Before my index finger and my thumb flipped open Darling's wallet, I made sure to remember its exact position on the table. An old hospital identification card was neatly placed under the clear protector slot.

Noah Jacob Lessor...

I tried not to gasp, but I couldn't stop the visceral reaction. Closing the wallet, I ran back to the couch. How did I not know it was him? I should've put the two together, but I hadn't, especially since Noah called, luring me to the curb right before the gold van pulled up demanding I get in. Was this what survival mode was? I thought as hard as I possibly could, but the only picture I'd seen of him was from the psych ward, where his hair was long and disheveled and his cheeks were sunken in. Back when the photograph was taken he wore a full, straggly beard, his eyes were loopy, and his skin was ashen. The man before me was, albeit insane, but well-groomed, a decent weight, and seemed physically healthy. The person from the snapshot in the case file had lost his mind. A huge difference in appearance existed between the two versions. Closing his wallet and returning it to its original location, I sprinted back to the couch. Not knowing what my next move was, Noah exited the bathroom.

"My dear?" he called softly as he towel dried his locks.

"Yes," I said, sitting up.

"How are you feeling? Your prescription will be arriving shortly. Would you like some supper or would you rather wait until the medication kicks in?"

"I'm okay. Thank you." Standing, I folded the blanket and returned to the table. Taking two place settings from the drying rack, I laid them out.

A snapping sound coming from the side of the shack

caught my attention. The sun was setting, and since we were in the woods, often I'd hear critters come to life around this time foraging for dinner, but this felt different.

"Is something the matter, my dear?" Noah asked.

"No. Not at all." I lied.

My gut instinct warned me that something was up. The little hairs on my arms stood on end. Unsure of what to expect, more than likely it was *she* dropping off my pills, I positioned myself away from the front door just in case it wasn't. Usually, she'd place whatever bags she had on the porch, then flee like a thief in the night. An unsettled edginess surged within me. With tremendous caution Noah examined my body language. Before he could utter a single word, a loud crash slammed through the air. A blur of people infiltrated the room, stunning not only me, but Noah as well. It took a hot second for me to realize one of the men was Luca's brother. Marco grabbed me and ran his hands over my face and body.

"You're okay, Maddy. I got you. You're safe," Marco said as he shoved my body behind his.

"What's happening?" I demanded.

Out of nowhere, Luca pushed Marco aside. He took hold of my frame and dragged me to the door. I begged everyone in the room to not hurt Noah. He was mentally ill and required help, not a beatdown or a bullet to the skull. This wasn't his fault. It was *hers*. Their focus needed to be on her, not Noah. The next thing I knew, Noah had grabbed Tony's gun and shot himself. Blood splattered everywhere as his lifeless form fell to the floor. Luca shielded my body with his, forcing my eyes away from the graphic, gory scene. A hushed, eerie silence fell over the space.

"We got Maddy, *Zio*. She's alive. The psycho offed himself. What do you want us to do?" Jimmy said into his cell phone.

I could hear Luca's father's voice on the line, but I couldn't make out exactly what he was saying.

"You got it, boss," he said and hung up. "Take Maddy outside while we clean up. Don't call anyone. Don't go anywhere."

"Come on, Mads," Luca whispered, continuing to use his frame to block my view of Noah.

Doing as told, I let him guide me from the shack to where a white minivan was parked. For several long moments he held me close. The sound of his steady heartbeat provided me with copious amounts of comfort and relief.

"It's over," Luca mumbled repeatedly.

"I'm okay, babe," I said, pulling away slightly from his grip. "Noah didn't hurt me."

"I don't know what I would've done if I lost you, Mads." Tears fell from his eyes. Never in all of the years that I knew him as friend or intimately had he cried. To witness this powerful, strong man weep broke my heart. I was aware that he loved me, but that moment revealed to what extent.

Pressing our lips together, I kissed him with all of the passion inside of my soul. As Luca grasped me firmly in his arms again, my hands felt the outline of a handgun tucked inside of the back of his pants. Before I could process what that meant and the severity of him possessing a weapon, because typically he always resorted to the use of fists to end confrontations, Frank and Salvatore arrived.

"You okay, Maddy?" Salvatore asked, touching my

shoulder lightly.

"Yes. Thank you," I said, placing my hand over his.

"The car is running. The doors are open. The kid is in the backseat. Keep an eye on him," Frank spoke hurriedly as he sprinted into the shack with Salvatore hot on his heels.

"Kid? What kid?" I ran to the vehicle the two men pulled up in. In the back, a male child no older than two was securely tucked into a car seat, wrapped tightly in a blanket, sleeping.

"Sarah's," Luca clarified.

"Where is she?"

"She *was* at the house Warren Lessor owned—the one he used to stash all of the people he abducted in. I'm not sure where she currently is, but I wouldn't press the issue," he said. A glint of warning flashed from his deep, brown eyes.

Nodding, I turned my full attention to the child. His little body stirred. Opening the car door, I removed him from the seat, and positioned him on my right hip. A bag rested beside him. Using my left hand, I found a sippy cup filled with juice. He happily accepted it, giggling.

"*Tesoro*, you're with Salvatore and me. Bring the kid. Luca, you go with Marco, Tony, and Jimmy. Call me when you're finished. We'll tell you what to do next," Frank informed us after he exited the shack.

"What's going on?" I questioned.

"Let me worry about that. You've been through enough. Give your *fidanzato* a kiss goodbye. You'll see him again in a few hours," Frank assured, sliding the door of the minivan open. Clutching the child against my chest, I turned to face Luca.

"Listen to my father, okay?" he requested, though a

certain amount of skepticism hung from his expression.

"Luca…"

"Please, *Vita Mia*. For me. Please," he urged, leaning in, and kissing my lips. "We have to move, now, but I'll see you soon. I love you."

Getting into the minivan, I watched Luca return to where Marco, Tony, and Jimmy loitered. Granted, a lot of heavy shit went down since I'd seen him last, but something about him was different—off. If pressed to determine exactly what, one might suggest Luca had embraced his heritage, his birthright. Standing beside three known Santino Capos, he fit in, perfectly. Honestly, I didn't know how to feel about that.

Once the minivan merged onto a paved road, Salvatore spoke. "You doing okay back there, Maddy?" He turned to face me.

"He didn't hurt me," I said, still processing recent events. An hour ago I was being held captive, now I was with Luca's family going who knew where.

"That's a good thing, but you're still going to need to be checked out by a doctor. Are you hungry? Thirsty?"

"No. Thanks. I'm good, Salvatore." Holding the child tightly, I stared out the window. The two men exchanged a quick glance.

"This is how this situation plays out. We're going to drop you off a few blocks before the local police station. You're going to run with the kid from where we leave you to the cops. The second you get there, tell them who you are. There's a missing person report on you—Luca filed it. The story you're going to tell them is you were abducted outside of my house. The man who took you brought you to the shack in the woods. Sometime this afternoon, a woman came by with a child. The man and woman engaged in a verbal altercation which became physical. While they were distracted with each other, you grabbed the kid and ran out of the house and didn't stop running until you got to the police station. Got it?" Frank said.

"Yes," I said. Most of the story was factual. Though I wanted to ask why not tell the truth, I held my tongue. Being caught somewhere between grateful, confused, and panic-stricken is a pretty tormenting place to reside, even if just temporarily. Adding a child to the mix magnified everything by a million and one. Whatever Frank and Salvatore needed from me, I'd do.

"Good girl. We keep family safe, Maddy, even if that means having to lie to the authorities from time to time," Salvatore added, obviously seeing the concern in my eyes. "If you go in saying what really happened—how the boys found you—you'll take us down. Luca included. He doesn't deserve that after busting his ass to locate you, all while being a stone's throw away from getting arrested because the police were trying to frame him. That kid has been to hell and back this past week. He practically lost his damn mind over being without you."

Slowing down, Frank stopped the minivan. "You run straight down this street into town. The closest police station is about half a mile from here. It shouldn't take you any more than twenty minutes on foot. There are no cars on this farm road, no cameras either, so don't worry about anyone seeing us. I'd take you closer, but I need you to work up a sweat in order for the story to stick. You can tell them it was Noah Lessor who abducted you and how Sarah Davis was involved, that they're both persons of interest in a case you've been investigating, and where he took you, but keep your answers short—especially the ones that bend the truth." He paused. "This is some scary shit. I completely understand how you feel, but no daughter of mine is weak. You're a Santino. Act like one. Channel the badass woman I know you to be and make this old man proud. Now, go."

"Thank you," I said, squeezing his biceps.

"You're welcome. We'll touch base later."

After I exited the vehicle, Frank turned the minivan around and took off back in the direction of the house. A sudden crash of thunder followed by buckets of cold rain poured from the sky. Running as fast as my legs would carry me, I made it into town. Upon getting there, I spotted the police station. Entering, panting, soaked to the bone, sweat dripping off of my face, practically falling to the floor under the dead weight of the child and the killer stitch in my side, I prayed someone would notice me, and would offer immediate assistance.

"Can we help you, ma'am?" A female officer inquired, getting up from behind a desk.

"Yes. Please. My name is Madison Langmore and I was abducted." I slumped to the ground, gripping the now screaming child to my chest.

Chapter 17

Frank

"The boys are gone." Salvatore moved away from the bay window and back to where I stood.

Sarah sat in an old armchair, clinging to her son. Dragging a nearby stool, I positioned it in front of her, taking a seat.

"It's just us, Ms. Davis. We're all alone in this great, big, old house out in the middle of nowhere. You've got some choices. You can attempt to run, though I can promise you won't get too terribly far. Don't let my age and his overweight stature fool you. We're both rather fast sprinters. You could scream, but no one's going to hear your cries for help. You could continue to sit there saying nothing, but that won't work for too long because we have ways of getting information out of people. Or, lastly, you could try to kill us. We wish you the best of luck with that. Many have tried, none have succeeded," I spoke as calmly and as casually as possible.

"I'd like to put my son down for his nap in the living room." A certain innocence resided in her wide, warm, brown eyes, but a tremendous hint of crazy danced inside of them as well.

"We're not stopping you." I stood, cueing Salvatore to follow her.

Uneasily she rose, cautiously walking into an area off to the left of the kitchen. What we were going to do

163

with her remained an unknown. How much she knew and how much she didn't was also a mystery. She wouldn't be forthcoming with simple scare tactics. Extracting her wealth of knowledge would take some assurances and a shit ton of finessing, something I didn't have the time or patience for at the moment. Maybe once Marco called I would depending on what was said, but for now, everything remained in a state of limbo. Moving through the space, I noticed no personal touches had been placed anywhere. Usually new parents displayed tons of snapshots of their children, but not a one could be found. My fingers flipped through several papers that were resting on top of an old-fashioned secretarial desk until a sudden crash caused my body to pivot sharply. Inaudible sounds of distress were coming from the back of the house where Sarah had gone. Bolting to the kitchen I found Sarah waving a cleaver at Salvatore while screaming a string of obscenities.

"Put the knife down," I said.

"Screw off," she yelled.

"Come on, Ms. Davis. Give it to me and we'll sit down and talk this out."

"Yeah, okay," Sarah said laughing like a lunatic, but I couldn't blame her. I wouldn't have believed me either.

"Don't do something you'll regret," I urged, slowly approaching her, making sure to keep my hands where she could see them.

As fast as a falcon, she lunged at Salvatore. For a slight woman she had a lot of strength within her core. Within a few seconds flat she had him pinned, and was straddling his rather large body. Salvatore struggled attempting to flip her, but after a moment he was able to gain total control over the situation. Holding her armed hand down didn't stop her one bit. She clawed at him with her free fingers. Grabbing a wad of her hair, he slammed Sarah's head into the tiles, knocking the psycho out cold.

"That bitch is crazy," he said through labored breathing. "One minute she's handing the kid a cup of juice and covering him, then the next she spins around with a freaking kitchen knife."

"Are you okay, Sally?"

"Yeah. Just got to catch my breath." He stood.

"We have to figure something out, and fast," I said impatiently. "If we let her go, she becomes a high-risk liability. She could head to the police and tell them what happened. She's got enough of your DNA under those long nails of hers to make the story stick. If we keep her with us, what do we do with her? Where do we stash her, and for how long? If we kill her, we'll never get answers if the boys can't find Madison or Noah."

"We've got the house in Queens. We could slam her ass there for a little while. The boys can keep watch over her temporarily. After we get what we want, we'll have to figure out a plan of attack, but that's something to worry about later. There's no way we can cut this woman loose, Frankie. She's a nut cake. If she doesn't rat us out, we'll have to keep tabs on her for the rest of our lives and then some. Whack jobs like this one seek revenge, and they don't rest until they have it. You know that."

Realizing Salvatore was right and no other choices presented, I spoke again. "All right. Go find some zip ties or rope, anything to tie her up with. See if you can locate a roll of tape for her mouth too. We'll bind her, then shove her in the trunk. The Queens safehouse is a few hours away this time of day. Chances are she'll remain knocked out for a while."

No sooner did I utter my last word, the lunatic stirred. She jumped up, snatched the cleaver from the floor, and ran toward Salvatore. Without hesitation my right hand retrieved my weapon from my shoulder holster. My index finger instinctually pulled the trigger of my father's Smith and Wesson Model Nineteen Revolver, firing one shot, nailing Sarah clean between the eyes. Upon impact, her body shoved back, finally falling to the ground with a loud thud. Instantly, blood pooled under her head.

"Problem solved, Frankie," Salvatore said.

"Problem solved my ass, Sally. Now we have to clean this shit up. Damn it," I hissed, removing my jacket, rolling up my sleeves, and opening the kitchen cabinet beneath the sink, looking for any cleaning product possible. "Start wiping crap down," I ordered, throwing a rag and a small bottle of bleach at him.

"What about the kid?" Salvatore asked.

"Doesn't he belong to Nick Winters? We'll get him to a hospital or we'll drop him off on Winters' doorstep."

"Whatever you say, boss."

Heading into the kid's room, something to the right caught my eye. A slightly ajar door to the laundry room piqued my interest. Opening it further revealed neatly pinned black and white photographs of dozens of people. Some I recognized like Madison, Luca, other members of my family, Salvatore, the Winters family, and myself, but others I had no idea who they were. Canary yellow Post-its had been tacked under the pictures. Illegible words were scribbled on each piece of paper. A red X was drawn over Madison's face.

"Sally," I yelled. "Get your ass in here now."

"What?" He entered, reeking like Clorox. "What the hell is this?" Moving closer to the images, his thick fingers inspected everything on the wall.

"Change of plans. First, look for anything important—paperwork, legal documents, anything at all. Grab it and toss it in the trunk of her car. Second, we bleach her fingers to remove your DNA from under her nails, then bag her up and toss her in the trunk as well. Third, call Arthur Lawrence. Fourth, we clean up the blood. Fifth, we take the kid outside. Sixth, Lawrence burns this horror house to the ground. Got it?" I instructed him, ripping the pictures and Post-its off the wall.

"You got it."

Rifling through drawers, closets, and cabinets, we filled three trash bags with various odds and ends. After getting Sarah's body into two giant contractor garbage sacks, we each took an end, and carried her corpse outside. Removing the spare tire, Salvatore and I crammed the papers into the empty well, placing her body on top. Slamming the trunk, I went back inside for the kid. The little boy stood in his playpen, staring blankly at me.

"Don't worry, *bambino*. You'll be safe and sound soon," I said softly. I located a diaper bag and stuffed it with a few diapers, cloths, clothes, and pacifiers. His green eyes watched my every move. Lifting him, I carried him into the kitchen where I retrieved a juice cup and a bag of cereal.

"I'm ready to blow this bitch up whenever you are, Frankie. Lawrence should be arriving any minute. The blood is gone," Salvatore said.

A buzzing in my pants pocket caused me to pass the

child off to Salvatore.

"Yeah, Jimmy."

"We got Maddy, *Zio*. She's alive. The psycho offed himself. What do you want us to do?"

Oh, thank God.

"Get her and Luca out of the house. They're not to go anywhere or call anyone. You, Marco, and Tony start sweeping the place. If you find anything incriminating or suspicious against us, take it. Wait for your father and me to get there before you start staging anything. There was an unfortunate incident with Sarah Davis that needs to be handled. We may as well kill two birds with one stone. After we drop her body off by you, you're to make it look like a murder-suicide. Just make sure you wipe everything down. You know how to do this. We'll fill you in on the story we're running with when we see you shortly. Once everything is settled, I need you and Tony to visit Arthur Lawrence. He's off duty, so go by his house after dark and pay him off. There's cash in your father's basement safe. Take fifty thousand. Understood?"

"You got it, boss," he said before hanging up.

"They found Maddy. She's alive and the boys are fine. Noah Lessor killed himself though," I conveyed to Salvatore.

"The boys know what to do?" Salvatore questioned, bouncing Davis's kid against his stomach.

"Yeah."

"Hello?" A familiar voice called from the front door.

"Chief Lawrence. It's good to see you. How've you been?" I asked, approaching him and shaking his hand.

"Living the dream. Whose kid?"

"Don't ask."

"Fair enough. What do you want this to look like?" His squinty eyes surveyed the structure of the house.

Arthur Lawrence was the Chief Fire Marshal for Nassau County. He'd been a friend of my father's. How the two men came to know the other I have no idea. It doesn't matter either. What did matter was he was a useful ally, especially during times like this. He'd set the house ablaze destroying all evidence and make it look like an accident. Nobody ever challenged his work. Granted, he came at a hefty price, but he was worth every penny.

"A kitchen fire started on purpose," I answered.

"Got an area you want me to concentrate on while I'm in there? Any bullets?"

"One bullet. Salvatore will show you where. Dealer's choice on how it begins. How long will it take to get the whole house up in flames?"

"You need it done fast?"

"As fast *and* accurate as possible."

"Are you challenging the work I've done for you and your father in the past? Have I ever done a shoddy job? Have you or anyone in your family ever been pinned to anything, ever?" Lawrence snapped.

"My apologies. This situation came out of left field and is a little too close to home, if you catch my drift."

"Your children involved?" His attention returned to the lay of the land.

"Something like that," I said, unwilling to divulge too much information. He was on a need-to-know basis.

"I'll use an accelerant. I can have this place engulfed in fire in about twenty minutes, tops. It's an old, wood structure, and it's been a particularly dry week. I'll also make sure to wash away any footprints or tire tracks out front in the driveway. Is that good enough?"

"Sounds great. Call Salvatore when it's done. Jimmy and Tony will swing by your place later, after dark, to drop off an envelope. I assume your typical rate applies?"

"Of course. Not a problem. Mary Alice is still at our daughter's house upstate. She had the baby last week. She stayed, but I came back because of work, so I'll be alone. The guys can come anytime. Have them use the back entrance. Oh, and please thank Gina for the baby gift. It was rather generous."

"Your family is our family, Arthur," I answered, patting him on the back. "We're going to get going. You'll handle getting the local fire department here?"

"I know a guy I can call. Don't worry about that. I'll text Sal when the deed is done."

With a nod, Salvatore and I took off. Focusing on the road and the GPS directions, we drove in silence. Finally, about halfway to the second location, Salvatore opened his mouth stating the obvious.

"Hey, Frankie, we're almost there and we still don't have a story."

"I'm aware." Pausing, a thought developed. "Davis blew up her house, maybe out of fear of being found out or the paranoid thought someone was onto her, then drove out to see Lessor. Perhaps to tie up loose ends. She's got a kid, so she takes him with her. She and Noah engage in a verbal argument which turns physical. Madison—barring she's not physically stable enough, grabs the kid and makes a break for it while the two are duking it out. Since Lessor offed himself, we'll have the boys drag Davis's body in and make it look like he killed her, then took himself out. According to the GPS, if we take this farm road the other way, it leads to a small town with a police station. Since we've been on this stretch I haven't seen a single car, and the houses are all set a ways back. We're in the middle of farmland. Cornfields for miles. Not a camera in sight. We'll drive Madison and the kid to the outskirts of town and have her run to the cops. Luca filed a missing person report, so when she shows up and tells them the story, they'll investigate the shack. Her account will align with what the police see, and we should be in the clear. Thoughts?"

"Sounds pretty solid. Do you think Maddy will go along with it?" Salvatore asked.

"She loves Luca. She will. Madison isn't going to want to see him get into any trouble, especially since he's the one who found and saved her."

"Are you sure?"

"Can one ever be one hundred percent sure of anything, Sally?"

"What happens if she doesn't fall into line?"

"If you're even considering what I think you are, forget about it. You'll destroy my son. If she puts up a fight, Luca will handle it. He'll convince her. If he can't, he decides how it plays out. Not you. Not me. Him, and him alone. *Capito*?"

"Yeah, yeah. And, what if she agrees, but ends up telling the cops a different story?" Salvatore lit a cigar.

"She won't. I know Madison. The girl is like a daughter to me and Gina. She'll do the right thing."

I hope. I pray. Because once she's at the hospital getting checked out, Richard and Donna Langmore will be there asking her tons of questions. They're private investigators whom I'm sure have been digging into where Madison disappeared to. With little to no idea of what they know or found, this could very well blow up in our faces. Added bonus, they believe my son has something to do with this and would love more than anything to pin this on him, thus on us. The one meal I shared with them that one time Gina invited them over was three painful hours of them looking down their noses at my family, especially my son.

"First things first though, Sally. Let's make sure Madison is strong enough physically and mentally to handle the task at hand. If we have to change the plan, we change the plan. It won't be the first time."

Slowing down, dirt and gravel crunched under the tires of the cheap compact car. Straining my eyes to see what lied up ahead, I spotted the minivan and Luca holding onto Madison. To the naked eye she appeared fine—thank God. Now all I had to do was clean up the mess, hide the evidence against us, and convince an outsider to go along with being an accessory to murder. All in a day's work, right?

Chapter 18

Luca

"Pop the trunk," Tony instructed as he tossed me the keys.

Catching them, then opening it, a black garbage bag shaped like a body caused my frame to freeze in place.

"We've got no time for you to freak out, Luca. This is life. This is what it took to save your girlfriend. Build a bridge and deal with it. I don't know what happened back at the other house, or what made our fathers do this. Quite frankly, I don't care. They had their reasons, and that's good enough for me. If they want us to know, they'll share. If not, we don't ask questions. Would you rather it be Maddy in the bag instead of the psycho chick? No. So move your ass," Tony ordered, shoving me out of the way. Reaching down, he threw Sarah's covered body over his left shoulder and went back into the shack. Placing her on a throw rug, he used a pocketknife to cut the bag open. Inside was without a doubt Sarah Davis. Cause of death—one clean, through-and-through gunshot wound to the head.

The three men worked rapidly, speaking seldomly. Tony and Jimmy staged the house, while Marco wiped surfaces down. It was easy to see they'd done this many times over.

"The bodies are positioned wrong," I finally spoke up. "If you're trying to make it look like he shot her, then killed himself, she'd have fallen this way, over here. He and the gun can stay where they are."

Dragging her to the new spot, I ran the made-up scenario in my mind, recalling a crime scene investigation class I'd taken years ago. Adding the final touch of pooling blood behind her head by taking whatever red liquid remained inside of the bag, I examined everything again. Once satisfied, we backed out of the shack.

"Wait, the serial number on the gun will link back to Tony. It has to be registered to someone. State records will tie it to us," I said panicking.

"Relax," Jimmy chuckled. "Serial numbers are removed the second we buy them. And I promise we don't purchase them from local shops. The gun will never be traced to any of us. The cops will think it's a black-market buy. My father gave us the bullet your father used on the psycho. It's all been neatly planted. Tony is changing the license plates and VIN number, plus making a few modifications to Davis's car. It's the perfect crime. Come on. We've got to circle back to the other house."

"There's no such thing as 'the perfect crime,' *cugino*. I've been a lawyer for a long time and have yet to witness it. There are always holes, clues, or something that escapes the mind of the criminal."

"There's always a first time for everything, Cuz. You have to trust us," he assured me, grasping and squeezing my left shoulder.

"Why are we going back to Warren's home?" I asked, watching Tony scratch and dent the hell out of Sarah's vehicle. In all honesty, he appeared to be enjoying himself, not at all affected by what just went down.

"To do a quick drive-by. Pop's orders," Marco explained.

Fifteen minutes later, as heavy, soaking rain fell from the sky, we sped past Warren Lessor's former house of horrors—or rather, what was left of it. A fire raged from the collapsed structure, spreading out onto the property. Several fire trucks were positioned around the area, attempting to put the blaze out. My body went numb. All sense of reality ceased to exist within my soul.

"Hey, Luca. Stop spiraling. You didn't do any of this," Marco said, placing his hand on my right knee.

"It had to be done," I said, still not feeling any better.

"I don't know what happened with the girl, but the psycho we were dealing with offed himself. I'm rather familiar with the way Pop and *Zio* operate. They wouldn't have hurt her if she were innocent. Maddy and the kid are fine. That's all that matters. Think of it like this—the world is free from two deranged lunatics, both of whom abducted your girlfriend."

I nodded, turning to look out of the window, watching drenched farmland zoom by. My brain shut off, not stirring again until we arrived back at the diner.

"We'll talk later," Tony said. He and his brother left Marco and me in the alley where my father hid his sedan earlier. They were going to get rid of Sarah's vehicle. Our job was done. Opening the parked car's trunk, Marco extracted a large, navy-blue duffle bag.

"We've got to wash off and change. I hope you aren't too attached to the outfit you're wearing," Marco said.

"Right here?" I asked, looking around.

"Pop is friends with the owner of this dump. They

have a stall shower behind the kitchen. It's not pretty, but it will do."

Following him through the back door, he waved at an older gentleman before ushering me into a small room.

"Strip down to your underwear and wait for me to finish. Toss everything—shoes, socks, jewelry, anything currently on your body goes in that bag. Got it?"

"Yeah," I said, turning around the moment he dropped trou. I remained like that until he instructed it was my turn.

"What the hell with this soap?" I asked. Upon contact, my eyes instantly watered from the stink, and my nostrils felt as if they were on fire.

"Just use it and stop acting like a little bitch. It's the soap surgeons use before cutting someone open. It kills germs and gets rid of bloodstains. Basically, it keeps the cops from finding anyone else's DNA on us should we ever get caught. Make sure to scrub under your nails good, and don't forget to go at that beard of yours. Fibers and shit can get trapped in the hairs. The final step is flushing your nose with saline spray and using fake tears to clean your eyes."

Until recently, at no time had I ever thought much of Marco. Of course, I loved him. He was my older brother, but sadly, I always viewed him as an idiot. Armed with a GED and a career as a bully, there wasn't anything to ever look up to, nothing to strive to be or follow. But, here we were. He was firmly in sound control, paying attention to even the tiniest of details. Things I'd never even consider, Marco had covered.

"You ready, *fratello*?" Marco inquired.

"Yeah."

"What's with you?" He cocked his head to the right and examined my face.

"Thank you."

"For what?"

"Everything. Not only for what you've done here today, but for always having my back."

"Are we supposed to hug and cry now?" he retorted.

"You're an ass. Forget I said anything."

"Hey," he said, placing his palm on my left cheek and slapping it lightly. "I'm your older brother. I will *always* have your back. I will *always* take care of you. I will *always* do whatever is necessary to make sure you're okay. If you ever need anything, anything at all, or you find yourself on the wrong side of the law, you come find me—no questions asked. Let me go pay off Spiro and toss this bag in the incinerator, then we can head home."

"Why did you decide to work with Pop?" I asked once we were back on the road.

"Truth? Besides it paying more money than I'd ever make in a lifetime because we both know I'm not a bookworm like you, it's a good, solid job. There's so much more to it than what people think or see. Take what you just went through. The police were useless. They wanted to blame you, then call it a day. More times than you realize the law protects criminals because the cops are lazy as hell. We correct that. Pop doesn't deal drugs, doesn't promote violence, isn't into prostitution, and isn't a racist or a homophobe. He helps people who can't help themselves, without judgment. He's not like the gangsters you see in movies. He's one of the good guys. Pop rules our family fairly, just like Nonno did. I'm proud to be his son and I'm proud to work alongside him every single day."

"I want in." Without thinking the words simply flew out of my mouth. Marco paused before letting out a loud, deep belly laugh.

"I'm serious."

"You want to throw away your nice, cushy, seven-figure job at Dewey, Screwem, and Howe LLP so you can become a goodfella? Come on. It's been one hell of a long day. You're emotional. Sleep on it. In a few weeks, after shit settles down, if you still feel the same way, talk to Pop."

Had my cell phone not rung, I would've fought with Marco about my recent, spur-of-the-moment decision. However, that conversation would have to be placed on the back burner until later. Looking at the face of the device, the number on the display wasn't one I recognized.

"Luca Santino," I said cautiously, unsure of what fresh hell was waiting around the corner.

"It's Jennifer. I'm using Ryan's phone because mine died. Maddy is at a hospital in Montauk. I'm texting you the address." Pure joy radiated from her tone.

"Is she okay?" I asked, already fairly sure she was having just seen her roughly two hours ago.

"Yes, totally fine. You were right. She was taken by Noah Lessor. He stashed her in some run-down shack in the woods. Sarah Davis and her baby went to said shack earlier today. When the two got into some kind of physical altercation, Maddy grabbed the child and ran. From what I obtained from the police, the Lessor estate, which is Noah's property, was set on fire, and both Noah and Sarah were found dead in the shack, which is also owned by Noah. Preliminary reports suggest Sarah was staying at Noah's house, started the fire, then took off to pay Noah a visit. Apparently, Noah shot Sarah in the head, then died by suicide. At least that's how the scene appeared to the authorities. The detective I spoke with said this is an open and shut matter."

"Is the baby healthy?"

"As far as I know. Ally is on the phone with a judge ordering an emergency hearing to place the child in the Winters' custody until things get sorted out."

"I'm heading to the hospital. I'm sure I'll see you shortly," I said, clicking the end call button. A sigh of relief came out of my mouth. My father's plan actually worked. Madison and the kid were safe and well, and the authorities believed the story.

"I have to be with Madison."

"I'll take you," Marco said, tousling my hair.

Chapter 19

Luca

"Hey," I said, walking into Madison's hospital room. She'd been admitted for overnight observation.

"Hey, yourself." She motioned for me to join her on the bed. Physically, she appeared all right. Color had returned to her beautiful face.

"You doing okay?" I asked, gently adjusting the shoulder of her infirmary gown.

"I'm totally fine. A little shaken and fatigued, but for the most part good. Not a scratch or bruise in sight. I'm not malnourished or dehydrated either. Noah may have been mentally ill, but he never laid a finger on me." She paused and leaned closer to my ear. "I told the police what your father and Salvatore said to. We're all safe."

I stood, pacing the space. Too many sentiments raced through my entire body. Finding balance seemed impossible. Adrenaline coursed in ways I never conceived.

"I always knew you'd find me, Luca."

I didn't respond because I couldn't find the right words. Shit, I couldn't find any words at all.

"Babe, stop. Come sit with me," Madison urged.

Before I had the opportunity to make any moves or to say anything, the Langmores and Noel entered, ignoring me and swarming Madison's bed. As I slipped into the hallway, my eyes spotted Jillian Winters walking down the hall. Hoping she wouldn't recognize me, I lowered my head and started to turn in another direction. No such luck. She stopped dead in her tracks and approached me.

"I'm beyond thrilled to hear Ms. Langmore was found safe, and I extend my sincerest apologies for dragging both of you into my and Nick's mess," she said softly as she touched my forearm.

"No worries," I said flatly.

The highs and lows experienced over the course of one damn day had taken its toll on me, causing total exhaustion to be the only thing I could accurately feel. Perhaps a good night's rest would reset my brain, restoring lost clarity and peace. I wanted to thank Jillian for providing the addresses, but I couldn't. No energy remained within me to care. Besides, if gratitude was offered, it would blow the entire cover story. I didn't know this woman from a hole in the wall. Why would I place my trust in a stranger to keep the biggest secret of my life safe? I wouldn't. She was a Winters, therefore she was the enemy.

"You'll even out, Mr. Santino. It's all new and fresh. This time next year what went down today will be a distant memory for both of you."

"I'm sure." I nodded, forcing a smile.

"The baby is Nick's—in case you were wondering. Ally is filing papers so we can take him home. Jordyn will have an older brother. His name is Tanner, but we plan to change that. He was born at home, delivered by Noah. The birth wasn't registered with the state, which is why there were no records. A detective found a few photographs of him being brought into the world at Sarah's house in Queens. After I viewed the pictures, piecing it together was easy. They also came across a few other damaging bits of evidence proving she was the one behind the blackmail."

"Congratulations, Mrs. Winters. I'm very happy this worked out well for you and your husband," I said, turning to walk away.

"Shit happens, Mr. Santino. Good shit. Bad shit. All day, every day. We see, hear, and experience everything from the epic to the screw-my-life nonsense on a regular basis. If you think for one hot second I buy the story you and Ms. Langmore are peddling, well, I have a bridge I'd like to sell you in Brooklyn. You have nothing to worry about. Cops are sluggish. The tale that was spun is flawless. The authorities will accept it for face value, stamping the file with that big, red, rubber closed seal. I've done shady crap too, but do you want to know what's most important to me at this very moment? The fact that Nick, Jordyn, and now Tanner are all safe and sound, with me, right where they belong. I did what was necessary to protect them. You did the same. Sleep easy tonight. As for Ms. Langmore, if you love her, fight for her. Man up," she said in hushed tones, slipping me her business card. "I'm a phone call or email away if you ever need to talk." With that, she turned on her spiked heels and took off, filling the hall with the sound of her shoes clopping against the tile, leaving me standing there alone, still unsure over what to make of the current situation.

Reaching for my phone, my fingers dialed an all too familiar number.

"Hey, Pop. It's me. Can we talk?"

Chapter 20

Frank

I'd never been so thrilled to come home to an empty house before. With no desire to speak or deal with anyone and their bullshit, the silence was more than welcome. The current situation with Madison became a little too close for comfort. Thankfully, that nightmare had come to an end, but not without copious amounts of heartburn and grief. I had no idea of her plans with Luca. I hoped it turned out well for my son—he truly loved that girl, but the outcome now rested in God's hands. Even though a large part of me believed Madison would do the right thing, tell the story the way we'd instructed her to, a tiny, nagging piece of me suggested she wouldn't, and all of Luca's persuasions would fall on deaf ears.

There's nothing you can do about it. Wait and see. Worst case scenario, she rats us out, and you and Sally will have to deal with it—which you will, because you always do. Just more stress, sleepless nights, and a bigger ulcer.

A certain amount of comfort that Beau Winters and our previous ties to that crap, shady politician hadn't played a role in the abduction existed within me. On the flip side, it irked me beyond measure Luca had to endure something he never should've. Since that boy was born I knew he was special, better than us. And yeah, sure, I'll openly admit Gina and I favored him over Marco and the girls, shielding him from more, pushing him to be superior, but for what? For him to end up being an accomplice to murder?

"Please, God. Don't let that kid be scarred from this. He's a good boy who deserves greater than what he's been experiencing," I mumbled, wringing my hands together while looking up at the sky.

A note lying on the kitchen table from Gina informed me that she had gone shopping with the girls, and would be back in a few hours. The timestamp was from a half-hour ago. With Marco finishing things up with Salvatore's sons, it was safe to sit and relax for a bit. Dozing off on the recliner never felt so peaceful until the damn landline rang. Getting up, cursing in Italian, I answered it.

"Yeah?" I grunted.

"Hey, Pop. It's me. Can we talk?" Luca said. His voice was off in more ways than one.

Shit.

"Are you okay, *figlio*?" I asked cautiously.

"No. I'm not." The sound of tears brewing in his tone caused my heart to ache for my precious youngest.

"Why don't you come over? Your mother is out with the girls and Marco will be tied up for a while."

"Okay. I'll see you in a bit," he said before the line went dead.

"Damn it," I hissed, wanting to hit the nearest wall, but knowing damn well if I did, Gina would hand me my ass later, crime boss or not. Inside the walls of this home, it was her way or else.

Making espresso, I parked my ass at the dining room table and waited. About an hour later, Luca arrived.

"Sit. Talk to your old man," I encouraged. My

handsome son's face was twisted with pain, anger, doubt, hurt, and just about any other negative expression one could have.

"I can't sit, Pop," he answered, pacing the length of the room to the point he ran the risk of making deep track marks in his mother's Persian rug.

"Luca, stop. Focus. What the hell is going on? Is something wrong with Maddy?" I demanded. I stood and took firm hold of his shoulders. I was growing fearful she might've sold us out once she spoke with her parents and the jerk-off dentist.

"She's fine. She's at the hospital with her family and *boyfriend*. She told the story you and *Zio* concocted. The cops appear to have bought it."

"You two broke up?" I questioned, relieved Madison did the right thing, but annoyed over this new twist of events.

Poor bastard. After all he went through, for Madison to dump him was a cruel move on her part. She could've at least waited until the dust settled.

"I'm unsure of what Madison is thinking. I love her. I'm in love with her, and she knows that. I proved I'd move Heaven and earth for her. I did my job, and now the ball is in her court. Shit, I staged a phony crime scene to rescue her. I could lose my license and go to jail if anyone ever found out about that. But, when the Langmores and Doctor No Nuts waltzed into her room, I was shoved aside, so I left. Why bother? I'm not good enough for her anyway. I'm great to have a good time with, take her to bed, protect her, but that's about all."

"None of what you said is true. Madison, or any woman for that matter, would be lucky to have you as their husband."

"Sure. Whatever. That's not why I'm here."

"Then why are you?"

"I'm resigning from my job tomorrow morning. After that's done, I'll begin my new career, with you, working as your personal counsel," he answered. His tone was dead serious.

"Absolutely not. You've been through a lot, which is causing you to operate from a place of pure emotion. You believe you're unworthy of a woman's time and affections, and after what you've experienced today, you feel different about yourself. It's all totally understandable. However, I will not allow you to trade in everything you've worked your ass off for to become someone like me. This path isn't for you, and *I* don't want it to ever be." My once fierce son who made it well-known he wanted to make his own way in the world had crumbled. He saw himself as nothing more than the names he'd been called his entire life. To say this saddened me would be the understatement of the year.

"I'm not twenty-two anymore. I'm a grown man, who after living through this past week realizes this is where I need to be. Let me use my knowledge to help you and our family. Let me keep you safe and protected the same way you've always done for me my entire freaking life. I will not take no for an answer. This is *my* choice, *not* yours. Besides, your current lawyer, Joey Donato, is a moron who couldn't litigate his way out of a paper bag. How he's managed to keep any of you out of jail blows my mind."

I sighed heavily before speaking again. "You're the first Santino to go all the way in school, to actually make something of yourself. Don't throw that away." Looking at him all I could see was my father. The resemblance between the two men was uncanny, especially when they were fired up over something.

"Please, Pop. Allow me to use the Ivy League education you provided and my skillset to help you. This is what I want," he pleaded. Heavy, dark bags hung under his once bright, brown eyes.

"I'll talk to *Zio*, okay? But, right now, I want you to go upstairs to your old room and get some sleep. When was the last time you got a good night's rest?" I stood, pressing my right palm to his bearded cheek. "You need a shave, *figlio*."

"Yeah, maybe it's time to get rid of it," he admitted, placing his hand on top of mine. He was fighting with himself to not cry in front of me.

"What are you going to do with Maddy?" I inquired.

"I don't know." He paused. "Can I stay here for a little while?"

"Of course. This will always be your home. Your mother will be thrilled you're back. You can stay as long as you'd like. Forever, if that's what makes you happy."

"Thanks, Pop." He turned, heading for the stairs.

Watching my empty shell of a son walk away hurt like a bitch. My heart tore in two. I could solve any problem, big or small, and I'd be damned if I couldn't figure out a way to fix this.

Chapter 21

Madison

The damn hospital held me for three days before finally handing over discharge papers. Both my body and mind felt fine, but the therapist who came to evaluate me insisted I stay for observation to fully address the state of shock I'd endured. Maybe remaining there was a good thing, but my body craved to be in my own house. Yes, of course, there were tons of emotions raging inside of me which could've been dealt with from the comfort of home—not some unfamiliar, sterile environment. Part of me felt sorrow for Noah, but the other part was very aware he committed a crime. You play, you pay. Had the police been the ones to find me, they'd have arrested him, and this time he might not have been sent to a mental institution. Would he have still shot himself? I hadn't a clue in the world. There were far too many variables to factor in. Engaging in the what-if game wasn't healthy, and it got you nowhere fast.

For the seventy-two hours I was stuck in the hospital, my room turned into a non-stop train station. Family, friends, doctors, nurses, the cops, and even someone from the FBI—Agent Timothy Wilder, I believe his name was—all kept coming in and out. However, after Luca left, he didn't return. I tried calling him a few times, but he didn't answer. Worry grew. What if the police figured out the truth? One would assume if they had, the police would've questioned me again, but they hadn't. This theory was put to rest late one night when Frank Santino swung by for a visit.

"Your doctor says you're doing well," he said, handing me several large Tupperware containers and a beautiful bouquet of purple roses. "Gina is concerned about the food you're being served and if you're eating enough. She made all of your favorites." Sliding the bedside tray closer, he placed a fork on top of a napkin. "Eat. You're too damn skinny."

"Please thank Gina for me," I said, smiling warmly.

"Thank her yourself the next time you're at the house."

"I'm not sure when that will be, if ever." My eyes looked down as my fingers traced one of the plastic lids.

"Oh, yeah? Why's that?"

"It's nothing." I lied.

"Talk to me, *Tesoro.*" He pulled up a chair and sat. He reminded me so much of his son. The way his brown eyes softened, his head tilted, and his brows knit—pure Luca. The expression and word combination caused an involuntary pang of crushing pain in my chest.

"I'm unsure of what my next move is when I get sprung from here. I'll figure it out. Always do. Anyway, thank you, Frank. What you and your family did for me was above and beyond what anyone else ever would've done. My parents, private investigators, hit a dead end, but you didn't. You kept going."

"Why wouldn't we be there for you? You're a part of our family." Patting my leg, he grinned.

"That means a lot."

"Hey, chin up. Whatever you want is what happens next, but don't let what went down shake you into a state

189

of fear. That's no way to live. If you want to marry Luca, marry him. If you want to stay with the dentist, stay with him. Switch up career paths? Go ahead. Whatever the choice, you will always have my full support. You control the outcome of your life, not others. As for healing after experiencing a life-altering event, we're all here to help—me, Gina, Marco, the girls, but *especially* Luca. If more assistance is required, we'll find someone who can provide it, regardless if you're with Luca or not. For now, rest. Decompress. Take this time in the hospital to relax. Refocus the lens. All is well in the outside world. It's over and has been put to bed."

"I appreciate that. How's Luca?"

"Hasn't he been up here to visit?"

"No. He came by the day everything happened, but he hasn't been back since. He hasn't returned my calls or texts either." Admitting this out loud stung like hell.

"I'm sure he has his reasons, whether we agree with them or not." His brushoff clearly indicated he was concealing information. What? I had no clue, but Frank Santino definitely knew something, and there was no way he was leaving this room without telling me.

"What do you know, Frank?" I pressed, sitting a little straighter, and turning to face him.

"I don't know anything." He shrugged.

"Don't bullshit a bullshitter, Santino," I warned. Though this was a risky tactic due to the fact of who this man was, finding out what was up with Luca was of the utmost importance. Last we spoke, Luca appeared amped up and very unsettled, but his behaviors were written off as him coming down off the adrenaline high, much like myself, except I had a sedative coursing through my veins keeping me calm. He did not.

A throaty chuckle rolled out of his throat. He sighed and leaned back in his chair. "He's been staying with Gina and me."

"Why? Is he not okay?"

"Luca believes he needs to make a change."

"And moving back in with his parents is that change? I don't buy it. Swing again."

"This is a conversation you should be having with him, not me. It's not my story to tell, even though you'd like it to be."

"Make it yours to share, Frank. I'm not screwing around anymore. This is the last time I'm going to ask before I pull this frigging IV from my arm, break out of here, and show up on your doorstep. Try me," I threatened, placing my left hand over the wad of tape which secured the needle in my right wrist.

"He quit his job, put his house on the market, and is now living back home, working for me. Now you know everything I do about the situation. Happy?"

"No. Why would he do that? He was on the partner track for Newman and Associates. Luca had more billable hours than anyone there because he busted his ass day and night. And, moving back in with you and Gina, selling a house he was proud to be able to buy with cash, outright—something's not adding up here."

"There's no hidden agenda, Maddy. I promise. Sometimes we just need a change of scenery."

"Well, I do too."

"I thought you were unsure of your future plans?" He raised a curious eyebrow.

"I realize things with Luca and me are complicated, but I know you could use a P.I. Let me help you. My personal life won't interfere with whatever you require of me." All uncertainty over what would be vanished. The path forward suddenly seemed crystal clear.

"What the hell is wrong with the two of you *idioti*? Did you and Luca suffer massive head trauma this past week? You have a wonderful, lucrative career with your parents. One day you and your brother will own that business. It's a reputable source of income."

"My skills are untouchable and you know that, Frank. Besides, if it's good enough for Luca, it's good enough for me. You said I was part of your family. Prove it," I challenged.

"Oh, *Tesoro*, you still have a lot to learn."

"No, I—"

He raised his hand. "Here's what we're going to do. First, heal. Settle the mind and all of the confusion banging around like ping pong balls up there. Once you're back on solid ground, figure out your love life. The dentist, Luca, someone else, or no one else—settle the heart. Then, and only then, come find me. We'll talk about what happens next. End of discussion."

I wanted to press the matter more, but a night nurse entered needing to check my vitals. Excusing himself, Frank kissed the top of my head and whispered, "*Non preoccuparti, figlia. Andrà tutto bene*," before leaving.

****

"Are you ready, sweetheart?" Noel asked, zipping my overnight bag shut the following afternoon.

"To get the hell out of here? Uh, yeah," I said with a light laugh.

"Let's get you home. While you're showering, I'll order takeout. Your parents messaged me this morning. They're going to meet us back at your house. And Ally called. She told me to tell you the child, Tanner, is happy, healthy, safe, and with the Winters. The adoption process for Jillian began this morning. She also insisted you take it easy and reach out when you're up to it."

"That's wonderful to hear," I said, happy for Nick and Jillian, and thrilled that sweet little boy was okay. My soul prayed he wouldn't remember a moment of what went down. Doing one last sweep of the room to make sure nothing was forgotten, we took off.

****

"I'm okay, Mom and Dad. Thank you for being here, but I'd like to be alone. I didn't sleep well at the hospital. I'm completely exhausted and in desperate need of some peace and quiet. I'll call you tomorrow. I promise."

Please leave. Your asses have been parked on my couch for hours. I have zero desire to recall any details from the abduction, nor do I wish to pretend all is well, because it's not.

"Go upstairs and get some rest. Mom and I will stay down here. We planned on sleeping over in your guest room tonight anyway," my father said.

"That won't be necessary, Richard. I'll be here. If anything comes up, I'll reach out," Noel interjected.

"No. No one is sleeping here. I'm totally fine. Please, go home. Everyone will get a phone call tomorrow morning," I snapped. The fact they cared so much about me was touching, but not today. Every ounce of my body, mind, and soul was tired, cranky, and confused over everything.

"Are you sure, sweetie?" my mother asked. A concern-laced expression hung from her face.

"Yes. I really am."

"You'll call if you need anything?"

"Of course, Mom."

"All right. You've been through a lot. I understand and agree with wanting space." She smiled and tapped my father's shoulder.

Finally, after a prolonged goodbye, I watched their car pull out of the driveway.

"What would you like me to order for dinner?" Noel questioned.

It's time. You have to set him free. You don't love him, because if you did you wouldn't be obsessing over Luca. At some point Noel is going to propose, and you're going to have to decline the offer. Rip the dangling Band-Aid off before it's too late.

However, something else wasn't sitting right. Before I let him loose, I needed to know one thing.

"When you found out I was missing, what did you do?" I asked.

"I met with your parents and David. They'd already spoken with the police and were attempting to follow a few leads of their own," he answered. "Why?"

"Did you help them?"

"How? I don't know anything about locating missing people. That's their and the police's job. I gave a statement to an officer, which I hope assisted them in finding you."

"What did you say? What did you think? Better yet, who did you point a finger at?"

"What's this all about Maddy?" His tone and demeanor shifted from soft and sweet, to hard and serious.

"Did you blame Luca? His family?" I demanded, placing my hands on my hips.

"Why does that matter now? You're safe and

sound."

"Answer the question, please."

"Yes. Yes, I did. Who cares? He's an epic waste of space. The walking definition of a loser. The only reason Ally hired him is because of his connections, not merit. He's a thug destined for a life behind bars along with the rest of his classless, uneducated family. How or why you went slumming with him is beyond me. Furthermore, you're not working with him ever again. I had a little chat with Ally this morning. Even if he hadn't resigned there was no chance in hell I'd allow him around you anymore. Forget about him. Do I make myself clear?" Noel seethed.

With every spoken word my blood boiled. "Get. Out."

"Excuse me?"

"Get out of my house and don't ever think about coming back. How dare you. How dare you talk about Luca like that? If it wasn't for him, I'd still be missing. While you sat on your rear end waiting for the cops and my parents to locate me, he was out there searching. I don't give a tiny rat's ass what his last name is, or what his family does. What Luca did behind the scenes for me stretches far beyond what you'd ever do. I'm actually happy this happened because it opened my eyes. It's him. It's always been him and always will be. I'm sorry for wasting your time, but I can't continue living this lie. I can't keep being something I'm not, and I can't be with someone I don't love—someone I'll never be in love with." Confessing my hidden emotions to Noel was probably the most freeing thing I'd done in a long time.

"Fine. Enjoy visiting day at Attica. I thought you were better than that," Noel hissed. "And to think I was going to propose."

"You thought wrong, and I'm so glad you didn't," I said.

After a brief, icy exchange, he turned on his heel and left but not before slamming the door. The surge of emotions I experienced when breaking up with Noel caused my already acute exhaustion to kick up in full force. Changing into my pajamas, I headed to bed, where I tossed and turned for several hours while attempting to sleep. My body craved rest, but my brain refused to allow me that simple pleasure.

Well, at least you got your heart in order. You know what you want. Too bad Luca's not on the same page...again.

My fingers stretched for and fiddled with my cell phone. I debated calling him. A part of me wanted to hear his voice to make sure that he was all right, but the other part was pissed. How could he not reach out? This was a man who adamantly declared his love and desire to get back together with me not too long ago. Hell, he even went as far as to propose, but he couldn't send a simple text? He put his life on the line to find me, and now suddenly he didn't give a damn? It made no sense.

Let it go for tonight. Frank said Luca was dealing with making changes of his own. He went through hell recently—because of you. He may need some space and time. If he doesn't reach out by the weekend, call him yourself. Put on your big-girl panties and go after him. For now, get some rest. Lord knows you could use it.

Placing the device on the nightstand, I shut off the lamp. My consciousness remained in a state of either being awake or in a light doze for a long while. As much as I desperately attempted to power down my mind, I simply couldn't. Somewhere around two in the morning, a loud, sharp beep from my phone tore through the silence, jarring me back to reality. The message read, '*If you're awake, come outside, Mads. If not, I'll wait on the porch until you see this.*'

Throwing my hair up in a topknot, I reached for the cardigan on the chair in the corner. Making my way downstairs, I peered through the side window beside the door. Dressed in baggy, gray sweats and a tight-fitting, black, long sleeve T-shirt, Luca walked the length of the porch.

"Babe?" I said, stepping outside.

He didn't speak but rather took immediate action. Approaching me, he grabbed my waist. He drew me close before he pressed his warm, soft lips to mine.

"I'm sorry, Mads," he whispered, moving away slightly.

"What happened wasn't your fault. You leaving the hospital never to return and ignoring my existence is," I answered, turning away. Tears of anger and hurt over his actions bubbled up, stinging my tear ducts.

"I did, many times actually, but Doctor No Nuts was always there. What was I supposed to do? Start another fistfight, but this time in the middle of a hospital with cops around? Put more stress on you? I couldn't do that," he explained. His expression was caught somewhere between feeling like an epic jackass and frustration.

"You could've answered my calls or texts."

"And say what, Mads?"

"For starters, I love you. I miss you. I need you. I'm on my way to be with you to chase the nightmares away. Maybe share things with me like how you quit your job, or how you're selling your house, or how you're living back home with your parents, that you shaved off your beard and are now working for your father," I ranted.

"You're right. There's absolutely nothing I can do or say to defend myself. My actions and behaviors were wrong, and I own that. Being there for you should've been my top priority, and now all I can do is apologize and swear I'll never act that way again." A sad, puppy-eyed look draped across his face.

"I've heard that line of crap before, ignored it, and look where I am now. Back where it all began." I didn't want to be mean, but I couldn't help it.

"I'm aware and I'm in complete agreement that you probably shouldn't believe a single word that comes out of my mouth on the subject. Having let you down twice has destroyed all of my credibility."

"I like you better with a beard," I said randomly.

"Give it a few days. It'll grow back."

"I broke up with Noel," I added as casually as possible, hoping to get a cue from his reaction.

"Oh yeah? Why's that?" His response was too cool and even to analyze.

"He wasn't you. Why are you here?"

"Because if I didn't try one last time to convince you it's us, *not* you and Doctor No Nuts, I'd regret the decision forever. When you were missing it was without a doubt the darkest time in my life. I traveled down some horrifying rabbit holes. I committed acts I never thought my hands were capable of. At first, processing what happened consumed me, but the idea that I did what was necessary to help you overrode any lingering guilt or doubt. The entire situation opened my eyes to everything. I love you, Madison. You're my girl. If you give me another chance, I won't let go this time. Marry me. Let me be the one to protect you and keep you happy for all eternity."

I'd never seen him as vulnerable and honest as he was at that moment. I thought I had, but I was wrong. Getting down on one knee, he produced a green, velvet ring box from his pocket. His beautiful, brown eyes sparkled with hope.

Chapter 22

Madison
Six months later...

"You look absolutely beautiful, Maddy," Jennifer said, adjusting the back of my veil.

"Thank you," I said, smiling. If you would've told me last year that I'd be standing in the back room of a church a half-hour away from marrying Luca Santino, I would've laughed in your face, but here we were.

"I didn't realize Luca knew so many politicians and law enforcement officers," she added casually through curious laced words.

"Those are Frank's friends," I commented, distracted by a stray hair. Reaching for a bottle of spray, I went at it.

"How is he adjusting to private practice? I still can't believe he turned Ally down when she offered him partner."

"He's really enjoying the change of pace." In the past, I shared practically everything with Jennifer, but this time I couldn't, and it was driving her nuts.

The day after I'd been found, Luca tendered his resignation, to Ally's great dismay. In a bold move, she offered him a substantial raise and a partnership agreement. He declined without a second thought. Since then, he'd been working for his father, sorting things out, and acting as the family's legal counselor. As for me, occasionally Frank tossed me side jobs, but career-wise I remained a private investigator for my parents' company. A choice sat in front of me, though. With them wanting to retire by year's end and leave the business to David and me, I wasn't sure I'd accept the proposal. A loud rap on the door caused my mind to snap back to glorious reality.

"Come in, unless you're Luca. Then stay out," I said.

"Just your future father-in-law," Frank said with a laugh. "The girls are outside in the lobby lining up. You should get ready too, Jennifer."

With a smile and nod, she exited the space.

"You're stunning. My son is a lucky man."

"Flattery will get you everywhere, Frank. What's up?" I said, taking a seat on the crimson sofa that was shoved to the far side of the room. Something told me he wasn't here to pay me a compliment.

"For starters, I'd love for you to replace Frank with Dad, *if* you're comfortable with it. Same goes for Gina. If not, we completely understand. Second, aside from marrying my son, what are your plans for the rest of your life? Career-wise, that is."

"Well, *Dad*, I haven't thought much about it. You're aware my parents plan to retire soon and want to leave the business to David and me. I'm still unsure if that's what I want. Why? Are you here to make me an offer I can't refuse?" I smirked.

"Ah, another wiseass daughter to add to the mix, because my hands aren't already full with Gia, Marie, and Tina. But, yes, I am here to make you an offer."

"I'm listening," I said intrigued.

"We'll talk more after you come back from your

honeymoon, but I could use your help with a certain matter—a rather sensitive one."

"How sensitive are we talking?"

"Extremely. What needs to be done has to be executed quietly and quickly."

"Who's the target and what kind of information are you looking for?" If his expression hadn't been so hard and serious I wouldn't have been as concerned.

"The Winters family." He paused, holding his right hand up in his classic Frank Santino style. "As I said before, we'll discuss the particulars *after* you and Luca return from Hawaii."

"You do realize you're going after the most powerful politicians in Washington, right?"

"I'm aware, *Tesoro*, but don't forget that they're going up against me and my family—*your* family. However, before you agree, you must realize and acknowledge that once you're in this family the only way out is in a body bag. We don't divorce. We never speak to the Feds. We protect one another, and trust we have each other's backs. If you have a problem, you come to me, first, always. I'll figure it out from there. You take orders from me, and me alone. We don't discuss business with those outside of the Santino circle. If anyone asks what you do for a living, you tell them you're retired. That you stepped away from your parents' business to become a wife, and eventually a mother. I can assure you that neither you nor Luca will ever have an unanswered need or want. Financially you'll always be covered. When I'm gone, Marco is up and Luca will become his right-hand man."

"Does Luca know?"

"Yes."

"And he's all right with this?"

"Yes."

"I'm in." I'd never been surer of anything in my entire life.

"Welcome to the family, *Tesoro*."

Chapter 23

Luca

"Are you happy, *Mrs. Santino*?" I asked, sitting beside Madison during our wedding reception, kissing the top of her hand where the diamond infinity band I'd placed on it a few hours ago sparkled vibrantly under the bright lights. The entire day had been surreal—perfect. Well, the part before the ceremony where Madison's father begged her not to go through with it I could've lived without, but it wasn't anything a little mental editing couldn't erase.

"Very. You?" She smiled.

"I got to marry you today. How could I not be?"

The sound of a utensil clinking against a champagne flute followed by my father's booming voice requesting silence cut through the crowd of over three hundred and fifty people, causing a hush to fall over the room.

"My wife and I would like to thank everyone for being here today to help celebrate the union of Luca and Madison. As Luca's father, I have always made sure he knows how loved and appreciated he is. We're beyond proud of the man he's become and of all of his accomplishments. He knows how much he means to us, and how important he is in our lives. So, because of that, I thought I'd take this opportunity to sing praise for Madison, my *tesoro*. You look absolutely beautiful. From the moment Luca brought you home, we've considered you our daughter. Today just enhanced that sentiment. Being a part of our family means you will always be loved and protected, no matter the situation. Whatever happens, it's got to get through me first, and no one gets through me, *and* no one hurts my family." He paused, making firm eye contact with Madison. Raising his glass, he continued. *"Per cent' anni. Evviva gli sposi. Saluti."*

Standing, Madison walked over to where my father was and embraced him tightly. The two exchanged words before he kissed both of her cheeks. She was in. I could breathe again.

****

Six months later...

The months following the wedding were a chaotic blur. The day we closed on our new house we found out Madison was pregnant. Though this wasn't the life I saw for myself two years ago, I'd never been as content or felt as settled. When Madison's parents retired, she sold her shares of Looking Glass to David, and began working full-time for my father. Before agreeing to allow this, I needed assurances she'd be safe. Two weeks later, I became a "made man"—a "goodfella," as Marco called it. With that came the added pledge and declaration of protection for me and Madison. My job was simple. Keep everyone out of jail. There's far more to it, but that's the bottom line.

Life was good. Real good, actually. However, you'd have to be a real idiot to think balance and stability lasted for longer than a hot second. Unfortunately, the guard I usually kept up dropped. I could say it was a foolish move, but that would be a lie. The moments spent were priceless, until late one hot afternoon in the middle of

July.

Balancing groceries while placing my key in the front door, I entered the house. Madison was asleep on the couch. Fans and the central air conditioning were both going at full blast. She was in her fifth month of pregnancy and the heat made for many daily cranky moments. Not wanting to poke the bear, I hurried into the kitchen as quietly as possible. While I put the frozen food away, a large, tan envelope addressed to me sitting on the center island caught my attention. Once the sealed flap was torn open, a small, hot pink slip of paper and an eight-by-ten black-and-white photograph fell onto the gray, speckled, marble countertop. Glancing at the picture, I quickly realized that it was an all too familiar crime-scene shot. Noah Lessor was lying dead across from Sarah Davis. My heart pounded. An internal boil so consuming set my core ablaze.

"Whoever takes a human life shall surely be put to death." - Leviticus 24:17

Your father's wedding toast to your wife was rather touching, but it won't save any of you this time. I know what you did. You will pay dearly for it. Every last one of you will.

A word about the author...

A lifelong storyteller, JP Barry specializes in crafting heart stopping, compelling, unique, emotional page turners for a variety of genres. A New York native, Barry is always on the hunt for ideas for her next novel. When not writing, Barry enjoys spending time with her family.

Thank you for purchasing
this publication of The Wild Rose Press, Inc.

For questions or more information
contact us at
info@thewildrosepress.com.

The Wild Rose Press, Inc.
www.thewildrosepress.com